love with a vengeance

LEYA LAYNE

Trigger Warnings

This is, for all intents and purposes, a monster romance, and this couple is morally gray. While there is a happy ending, not everyone survives until the end book. To be respectful to those who need warnings and those who see them as spoilers, I have placed the trigger warnings on my website. Scan this code to check the site.

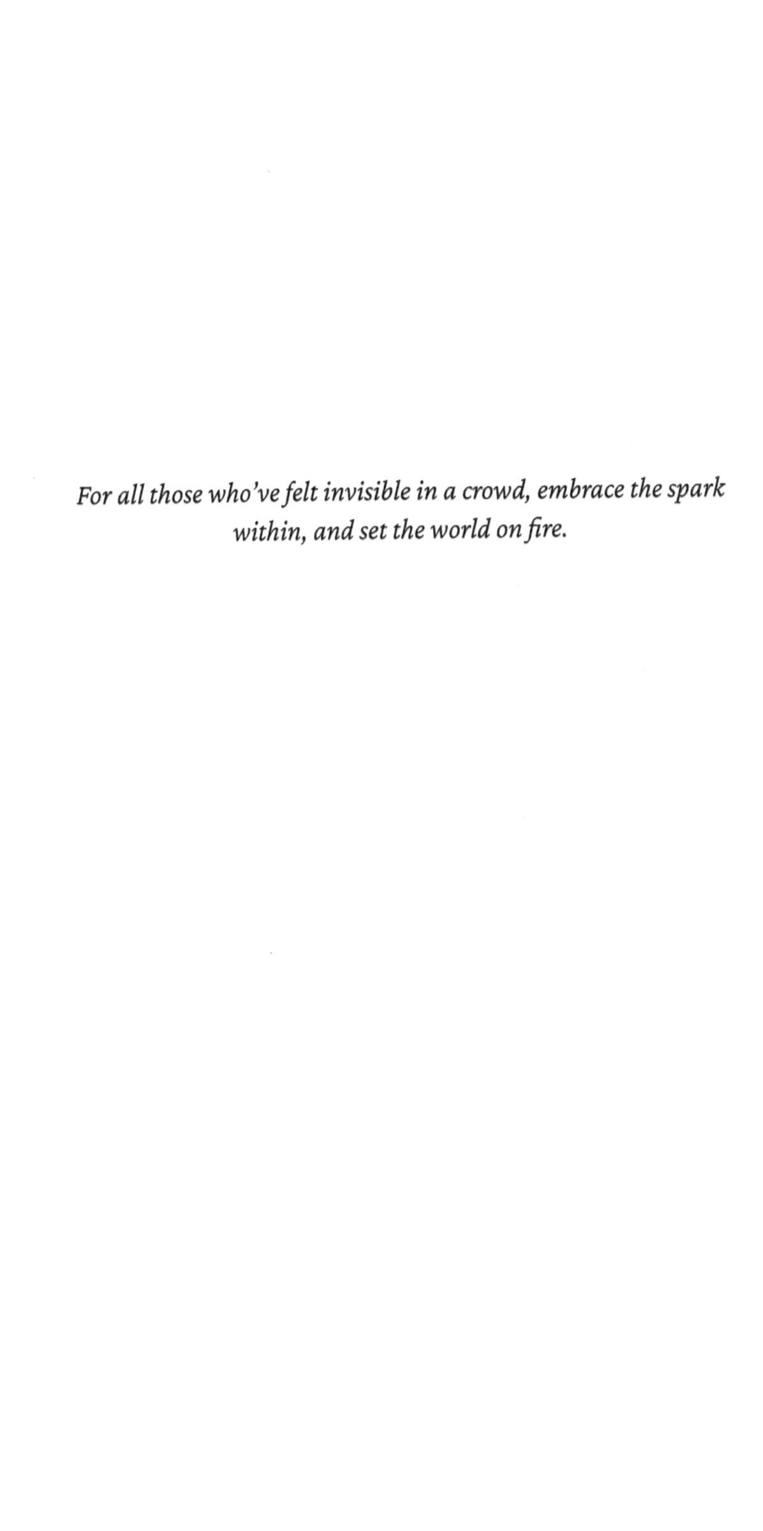

For all those who've felt invisible in a crowd, embrace the spark within, and set the world on fire.

I PASS through the sliding glass doors and up the escalator. For all the glitz and glamour the company promises, their entrance appears more like a warehouse of used goods than a cruise port, at least until we reach the waiting room. Our group is ushered into a makeshift chapel for the ceremony. I really don't want to be here, don't give two shits about this marriage, and I certainly don't want to be in the wedding party. My parents, always scheming to rise in the social hierarchy, insisted I accept the invitation. One look around the room at the haughty faces reminds me how much I've hated these people since high school. The idea of spending three days with them inside of a floating tin can turns my stomach. Still, I plaster on my well-honed smile and clap enthusiastically at the kiss that promises forever, knowing that both the bride and groom have separate lovers standing on either side of the aisle.

It's not that I'm a prude. I'm most definitely not. But, it is one thing to have a lover outside of your relationships and another to just swap around your inner circle. This crew might as well be swingers. I catch myself once again wondering why in the hell I'm here when I'm the odd man...er...woman out.

Then I notice another stranger in the room. He's wearing a suit that closely matches the rest of the groom's party, but he doesn't quite fit in. He's tall and handsome enough to be part of the group, but he doesn't have the air of privilege that has always raised my hackles.

He stands to the side, looking down rather than trying to keep all eyes on him. That must be what drew my attention in the first place. No one on that side has spoken to him, much like no one on this side has spoken to me. I spent time getting ready with them, dressing in the same hotel room, and riding along in the same hired van, but I was hardly acknowledged at all. My nose scrunches in disgust slightly before I remember where I am and school my face. I only have to play nice for a couple days. Then I can once again pretend they have all fallen off the face of the Earth.

As soon as the ceremony ends, we're sent off to check in for the cruise. The ship is imposing. We climb the ramp for what feels like forever, and yet it just keeps going up. I have to strain my neck to see where the top deck touches the sky. How do people not get lost on a ship this size? By the time we reach the lido deck, there are already what seem like thousands of people aboard. I grab a drink off the first tray I walk past, handing them my key card to charge my room.

Raucous laughter from the wedding party behind me says that I'm going to need more than one of these. All I want is to head straight to my room, strip out of this dress, and scrub this painted mask from my face, but the rooms aren't ready yet. Instead, I find a seat at the outside bar and suck down the hurricane before ordering another.

Normally, I love people watching. It is a wondrous process to see how others behave in social situations when they don't know they're being watched. The masks go on and come off multiple times. The sudden moments of relief or stark incredulity pass over their faces before they can cover the response. Rarely do their companions see what is happening. There's an emptiness in most public conversations. It is when two people are alone that they show their true natures. But, if one watches carefully enough, they can catch glimpses within the crowd.

Some might call me a cynic. Others might say I'm simply bitter that I was never fully accepted into this group of friends. Those who know me well, though, know that I have been studying the fakeness of human interaction for years, long before I earned a major in Sociology. Case in point, the rousing banter coming from the other end of the bar. Much like everyone else in the near vicinity, I turn my attention to the raucous crew. No one would ever guess that we came here together, and I'm hoping to keep it that way.

Suddenly, I feel eyes on me, watching me as intently as I've been watching the crowd. A shudder runs up my back. I find him in the shadow of the bar's awning, his dark eyes honed in on my face. Like me, he is out of place with the group. His suit, unlike the others, still looks freshly pressed. His hair remains perfectly coiffed, and his lips, his perfect, full lips are drawn in a tight line. When I finally look into his eyes, his brows draw quizzically together, and his lips part slightly. We are at least twenty feet apart with a throng of people between us, but it's as if I feel a puff of surprise leave those lips before they turn up in a sly smile. His eyes, however, don't change to match the expression.

I DON'T RECOGNIZE this woman, but I can't keep my eyes off of her. When I decided to attend this wedding for a man I've known for years amongst the lug heads I've hated equally as long, I imagined that every woman they'd have with them would be vapid and self-absorbed. This one, however, doesn't look through me like everyone else. Though I stood alongside the rest of the groom's party, no one acknowledged me. It was as if I wasn't there, until I felt her eyes on me. I thought it was a fluke, a trick of lights through the window when I felt her gaze land on me in the chapel. Now, it's undeniable. She's looking straight at me, head tilted to the side like she's trying to make sense of what she's seeing. We've never met, but I feel drawn to her.

Though she's wearing a face full of makeup, her hair dolled up like the rest of the bridesmaids, and in one of those ridiculously matching dresses, she stands out. The dress hugs her ample curves rather than falling lifeless off the others' thin frames. Her dark hair is a stark contrast to the various shades of bleached blonde and brown-to-blonde ombre of the rest of the group. My fingers itch to pull the pins from her hair and see her lipstick smeared from my kisses. She is simply...*bella.*

"Do you remember the last time we were on this particular ship?" A voice breaks my concentration, pulling my attention back to the group of men I'm with and yet couldn't be further removed from. A frown crosses my face as Jaison gives Arthur a wicked smile to match the one the other man had when he asked the question. Not everyone in the group responds with the same smile, which loosened the grip the question has on my chest.

"I bet we could have just as much fun if not more this time," Jaison says, not acknowledging the mixed emotions of his friends.

"Dude, we don't need a repeat of that trip," Greg inserts into the conversation, trying to deflect.

Arthur smirks. "We have some new blood this time, so we can make it even better." My brows crease low and a sneer crosses my lips as my eyes go back and forth between the two men who have always been the group's ringleaders. I don't like the way Arthur stares at the unknown woman who's held my attention all day. Something isn't quite right about this man, and the fact that she's in his line of sight means something doesn't bode well for her. My gaze locks with hers, uncertainty written on her face, likely at my changing expressions, and I wish I could ease her anxiety.

When the announcement is made that rooms are ready, she turns toward the other women without a second look at me. After a few exchanged words, she takes off toward the elevators. Five sets of male eyes, mine included, watch her exit through the sliding glass doors, and I take off after her. I am going to need to keep my eye on her and them if this weekend is going to go as smoothly as possible. We are all here for a reason, a celebration of sorts, and I won't let anything, or anyone, ruin it. Of course, there's also my curiosity about her, but I'll examine that later.

three

VETTE

I BARELY GET into the elevator and turn around when a man's hand, no, his whole body, slips through to join me. At least that's what I think I see happen. One second, the doors are closing, and I see a hand slide between them. The next second, the man I've been staring at most of the day is standing between me and the closed elevator door. I might've been afraid of his quick movements or the fact he followed me inside, except we're in a glass elevator. There isn't much he can do that won't be seen. Truthfully, though, it's not fear that's coursing through me when I look into his eyes and the way they take me in, like they see every inch of me and are still fascinated.

"You almost didn't make it," I say with a giggle.

He gives me a smirk and turns his head slightly to look back at the door. "It was nothing. I'm used to getting into what I want."

Tingles erupt low in my belly. His beautiful tenor voice holds a hint of an accent. Spanish? No. French perhaps? I shake my head slightly. That's not it either. His head tips to the side with a question. I laugh then, realizing that I wasn't keeping my thoughts as quiet as I should have.

"I was trying to place your accent," I say with a small shrug, a smile playing on my lips.

"I have an accent?" he asks with his own shrug.

My smile grows. "Well, you definitely sound different from your friends upstairs."

He opens his mouth slightly, grin still on his face, and I can see his tongue tucked behind his teeth. For some reason, that sight makes the tingles grow.

"I am different from them in a number of ways, Bella."

"Oh," I say, "Italian, it is."

At that, I'm stunned into silence at the most beautiful smile I've ever seen. His teeth are perfectly white and straight. His lips are still as lush as I had noticed in the chapel. I can hardly breathe. The man is stunning, and this elevator is moving entirely too fast.

"My name is Alessandro," he says with a small bow of his head.

"You can call me Vette," I tell him.

I reach out my hand to his, and he lifts his toward mine but doesn't immediately grab it. An unreadable emotion crosses his face as he looks at the two hands before tentatively touching his fingers to the pads of mine. Though I don't see them, sparks pass between our skin until he grabs my hand firmly in his, turning it over to place a kiss on my knuckles. His wide grin returns.

"It is very nice to meet you, and it's a shame our friends didn't introduce us. No matter. I have no problem following my interests."

His words both excite and repulse me. I pull my hand from his, suddenly questioning the reason for his interest. I've known his friends for years. Though I had judged him as being different from them in looks and poise, I wonder at what history they share, as I'd never seen him with them before. My nose wrinkles at his slow response, and when the elevator doors open, I try to push past him.

"Excuse me," I say, those tiny electrical charges tickle my skin again when I'm near him.

He turns to the side to let me pass, but touches my inner elbow, both halting my progress and making my heart stop. "Have I offended you?"

I swallow back a retort and simply say, "I need to go and get out of…" I gesture up and down at myself with my hand, "this." I can hardly form words with his hand on my bare skin. I'm sure he can feel my pulse vibrating at his touch.

"You don't have to fear me, Bella. I find you interesting because you appear different from everyone else I've seen in this circle."

Part of me starts to relax at his statement. Still, I'm afraid to trust it, to trust him. I certainly wouldn't trust any of them. I've seen their stares. I know the games they play with each other. Somehow, I've managed to stay out of their way. My goal is to do the same this weekend. I won't let this dark stranger, who seemingly appeared out of nowhere, cause me to fail.

"At least let me walk you safely to your door."

A silent huff escapes through my nose. I'm not sure I want this man to know what room is mine, and yet, I'd like nothing more than to invite him in. I finally exit the elevator with him at my side. My room is toward the front of the ship. When we were first told to contact the travel agent about booking our rooms, I specifically asked for one away from the group. When we checked in, and they tried to connect our rooms through the cruise's messenger app, so we could all be together for dinner, it wouldn't work. Constance was pissed that my room wasn't near theirs and that I wasn't readily available. I don't know what she thought. It's not like we've ever been close friends, and I'm not one of her minions she can have at her beck and call. Besides, we both know our parents are the only reason I'm even here.

I may have managed to keep myself separated from the group and safe from group texts and uncomfortable meals, but him knowing where my room is puts my solitude in danger. Still, there's something about him, about his demeanor, that makes me trust him more than the men he's here with, and probably more than the women as well. I have no doubt that should I fall from the top deck of the ship, only one of them might call for help.

When we get to my room, I quickly grab the envelope with my key card from the wall, hopefully before he sees my full name. It's not that I care whether he knows my name or not; it's that one of two things happen every time someone learns my first full name. They either immediately rush into a slew of questions about its origin and its meaning, or they want to know whether or not it fits who I am as a person. As if the names our parents choose for us truly decide our personalities. If the conversation wasn't so awkward, the absurdity of the assumption would make me laugh every time. Though, that outcome isn't the worse of the two.

The worst option is the unwanted nicknames that come from them knowing my first name. Odveta, a name sung from my grandmother's mouth like a beautiful melody, becomes a discordant cacophony of 'oddball,' 'oddity,' or the ridiculous sound play of 'aardvark.' Even worse are the guys, like the ones on this trip, who call me Odyssey when their girlfriends aren't around, as if I'm a conquest to be had, something epic to chase. I don't want to hear any of those names from his lips.

I tear the envelope open and pull out the card, ready to let myself into the room. "I'm safe now," I say, turning toward him. "Thank you for the company."

He is standing directly in front of me, and I have to look up to see into his beautiful topaz eyes. Those shockwaves still trickle through me at our proximity. He seems unaffected, but there's no way I'm the only one who feels this. I shake my head to purge those thoughts and turn to look at the door, ready to slip the card in and escape. His fingertips brush my chin, turning my face back to his, and I bite my lip involuntarily. He is so close I'm surprised I can't feel his breath on my face. Just as quickly as he had turned me toward him, he releases my chin and tucks a loose tendril of hair behind my ear. The movement is so intimate a shudder runs up my back.

"It was my pleasure, Vette. I suppose I should be getting back to the group."

"Yes," I say in a breathy whisper, far too affected by him. I clear my throat and try again. "Yes." My voice is much stronger this time. "I'm sure they're waiting for you."

He laughs at that, but it isn't a mirthful one. I don't have time to ponder that response, though, before he follows it up with "I'm sure I'll see you later." Those words hold something more like a promise than a simple farewell, and I clench my thighs together to stave off the response my libido is having. He winks and then walks away, as if there isn't arousal coating my thighs. I watch him leave and know how I'll be spending the next half hour alone in my room.

four

ALESSANDRO

IT WAS NEARLY impossible to walk away from her. The way her mouth opened and her breath hitched at my touch on her chin. I nearly forgot myself and covered her mouth with mine. The way she responded to my touch, *cazzo*, the fact that I couldn't stop touching her. I'm not an innocent man, but the things that I want to do to her, the images dominating my mind. They're carnal in a way I haven't felt in years. My body is alive with need. The feeling is so far beyond a wish or passing arousal. Touching her skin for the first time was like waking from a nightmare. It was a feeling of wholeness. Though I lost my faith four years ago, I have no doubt that if there were a heaven, it would be slipping inside of that woman.

Rather than wait for the elevator, I detour to the stairs and run up them two at a time. I need to expel this kinetic energy that had built between us. I also need to get back to the group and find out what they're up to. Specifically, I need to know their plans for Vette. I have no idea what her full name means or how it's pronounced, but it sounds beautiful in my mind. The way she'd quickly torn at the envelope with her keycard in it, kept me from asking or even acknowledging that I had seen it.

Maybe I'd get a chance to ask her about that once we were again alone. A smile plays across my lips, and I readjust myself at the thought of being alone with her. I want to feel more than the skin of her hand or her elbow. I want to attempt to taste her lips, if she'll let me. Something in the way her pupils dilated when I moved her hair made me think she'd let me try.

I return to the bar to find only Jaison and Arthur there. Somehow, they had already changed clothes from the well-tailored suits to comfortable linen shorts and t-shirts with their signature flip-flops. One would think they'd have upped their wardrobe game since college was over, but apparently these two weren't ready to let go of that era. They were the type to look down their noses at everyone and yet not grow up from living what they considered their glory days. Both of them had been on the wrestling team together in high school and college. The others had been on the high school team but gave it up to focus on their studies in college. That change in their dynamics, or rather the separation amongst the group is probably how the other two managed to turn out to be somewhat decent people, at least as decent as one can be when they know their friends are absolute shitheads and don't say anything because it benefits them.

I saunter up to the two men who ignore me as usual. They did the same thing the last time we all traveled together, ignored my existence until it benefited them. I still remember their huge smiles. *Alex, come join us...You need to loosen up, man... Have a drink...You, dude, how long have you been cruising?...I wonder where the staff hang out...That dealer is hot! I'd like to catch her in a dark stairwell.* I should have known then that I'd regret hanging out with them, especially these two. But I was young and naive. They always looked like they were having so much fun, and some days could get boring, even on a ship this size amongst all these people. I found myself constantly looking for the boisterous group until they let me into their circle. Arthur's voice breaks me from my reverie, and I look up in time to see the phone screen he shows to Jaison.

"So no one has found out what room she's in yet?" Jaison asks.

"That bitch has always thought herself better than us, always believed she was smarter than us." Arthur responds, his voice a mixture of disappointment and contempt.

"She'll come around. The girls will make sure of that. Besides, there are only so many places to hide on a ship."

Arthur's tone is diabolical. "She'll find out that when you come into our inner circle and take a spin on the wheel, we are the sure bet. The odds will never be in Oddball's favor."

I'm seething by the time he finishes his little declaration. These fuckers really plan to play a game with her. My chest tightens with concern wondering if she knows it. What if she really thinks those girls are her friends, and they're just setting her up? What if she trusts these dudes? Shit! I can't kick all of their asses, at least not when they're always together. That didn't work out well for me the last time I tried. I either need to find a way to keep her occupied and separate from the group or to get them to turn on each other. If they're all otherwise occupied, everything will go according to plan, the plan I created long before the ship embarked, before she looked into my eyes and touched the soul I thought was gone.

five

VETTE

I ENTER my room and quickly close the door behind me. My body is on fire from the heat between my thighs. It's like every spark from him fed a flame of desire that I can't control. I'm not a virgin, but I'm also not some lust crazy girl. There is just something about him, something, I don't know, needful that calls to me. I pull my dress over my head and throw it into the chair nearest the door. These rooms are tiny, smaller than most hotel rooms. I'm glad I got one with a balcony, else it might start to feel claustrophobic if I had no window or anything. I pop my bra off without any fanfare and throw it on top of the dress.

Before I can fall onto the bed where they've obviously pushed two twin-size mattresses together, my fingers are in my panties, rubbing circles on my clit. Thankfully, we're in the middle of the ocean, else someone walking by would get an eyeful since I hadn't bothered to close the curtain that leads out onto the balcony. I'm too needy. I don't even take the time to find the vibrator I hid in my suitcase when I packed for this trip. Instead, I flop onto the bed, drawing one knee up, fingers continuing to swirl at a rapid pace, pushing me further toward the precipice. My other hand finds my nipple, pinching and twisting until the sharp hint of pain pries a gasp from my mouth. I imagine his strong hands rubbing my most intimate parts, driving me toward release with his words of promise and a look in his eyes that matched the one he had before he walked away.

I don't remember falling asleep, but it's nearly dinner time when I wake. Shit, one more reason for Constance to be up my ass. I jump up, throw my hair in a messy bun, scrub the smell of travel off my body, and toss on the first cocktail dress I can pull from the suitcase. It's a short, gold number that compliments my naturally golden skin. A pair of strappy, black heels and small clutch complete the ensemble. I'm grateful I hadn't bothered to scrub the makeup from my face because I was just able to freshen up the look with some tinted lip gloss before running out the door. I can't believe I damn near let myself sleep through the promised cocktail hour. They would never let me live that down, as it's one of the few wedding-related events I promised to attend.

Apparently, ours was not the only group that paid for the event because when I walk into the lounge, there are people everywhere. I found our group of seven in the corner watching the rest of the crowd like conspirators on some secret mission.

"So nice of you to join us," Jaison says, sarcasm dripping.

"You almost missed the toast to our marriage," Constance chimes in.

I school my face and try to put on a contrite look for the group when I apologize. Arthur scoffs at my 'lost track of time,' and I shoot him a scathing look. I know I was sent here to play nice, but they make it very hard.

"Well, we're all here now," Tracy says, breaking the tension. "Let's get the celebration started!"

Everyone cheers, and I grab the last champagne flute sitting on the tray before I feel rather than see Alessandro join the group. How did I miss that he wasn't here? How did they not notice that a member of our party was still missing? A combination of guilt and doubt begin to slip in—doubt that they were really waiting for me if they could so easily forget someone else, and guilt that I had also missed his absence, especially considering how affected I am by his presence. He already has a glass of champagne in his hands that he tips to me in salute. He must've picked it up from one of the other trays around the room because I grabbed the last one from this tray. I guess I'm really not the only one who this group treats as invisible. I smile at his acknowledgment, but my smile is sad. It's a terrible way to treat a friend.

I don't have many friends, but I would never treat the few I do have like this. Honestly, I would never treat an acquaintance like that. I understand where they get it from, though. My parents behave similarly, which is probably why I don't have many friends. I can't trust people to be genuine and show who they truly are. Nearly everyone I've known my entire life has been two-faced, including those I love most. I look up from my drink to Arthur's lecherous grin, Alessandro no longer at his side. Disappointment starts to wash over me until the tingles start at my elbow and his voice comes from directly behind me.

"Is everything alright, Bella?"

I swallow, a smile spreading across my lips, and I turn slightly to see him standing right next to me.

"You know that you can pretend I'm not here also. Then we can both pretend we're here alone together without drawing attention from the others."

My pulse quickens, and I nod slightly when his hand touches my back where the dress opens. I shiver from the jolt of electricity.

"Are you okay?" Constance asks. "It's hot in here, and you're over there shivering." Her shrill voice grates on me.

"I'm fine," I say, looking directly in her eyes while trying to pretend his fingers aren't stroking the sliver of bare skin.

"I have a jacket if you'd like," Arthur says from the other side of the table, and Alessandro's fingers grip my waist possessively. Gregory watches the exchange and his eyes widen before he relaxes into the facade of nonchalance.

"No, I really am fine," I manage to choke out.

The other women eye me skeptically while the men just look me up and down. All I can focus on, though, is the man behind me, and the slow caress of his fingertips once he relaxed again. When the group laughs at something I don't hear, I chuckle along. In what seems like a flash, the guys finish off their second drink and excuse themselves to the sports bar, stating they wanted something a little more potent for the night ahead. I probably should've been paying better attention to the conversation because I have no idea what the evening's plans are. The tantalizing caresses and soft words of appreciation have me thoroughly distracted.

"I should probably go with them," Alessandro whispers in my ear.

It takes all of my strength not to moan at the sound of his voice that close. I turn my cheek toward him, and he gives a light kiss. I know I'm probably going to get a lot of shit if any of the women see, but I don't really care. I don't care about much of anything except the feel of his skin on mine. That and the extreme sense of emptiness I feel when he takes it away. A pit forms in my stomach like I just experienced the greatest loss of my life. Before I can turn to run after him, which is what my body urges, Tracy stands and grabs my arm, pulling me toward the door.

"Come with me to the bathroom. I know we're on a ship

and things are supposed to be safe, but I don't feel like going alone." She says that part aloud for everyone else to hear, but once we're out of earshot, she whispers, "You're acting strange. What's going on?"

"Nothing. I'm fine," I say before spewing my true thoughts. "You know I've never been comfortable with these whole group things. Constance is a bitch, and the guys, well…well…" I let out a strong sigh.

It's hard for me to say what I want to say about the collective of them when I think of Alessandro. I find it hard to believe that he is like the rest, which makes me wonder even more why he's with them. I turn to Tracy, ready to ask if she'd ever met him before this trip when she pulls me into the bathroom and pushes the door shut.

"Look, the more you act like you stand out, the more attention you get from them. They're like hound dogs, and you are constantly bleeding for whatever reason. I'm not saying they would do anything, but it makes Constance and the others…"

I finish the sentence for her, "feel like I'm trying to take their men."

She nods. "You're not the only one who doesn't fully fit in here, but we all have known each other for such a long time."

"I don't understand how you do this shit with them on a regular basis," I snarl. Her lips tighten into a pucker, and I know I've hit a nerve. I'm not mad at her. In fact, she's the only one of the group who I feel still has her soul. Some days, I wonder how she's kept it. I would sell mine to get rid of the lot of them. "I'm sorry, girl. It's just every time we're all together, I feel like we're back in high school. I already know they don't want me here."

"That's the thing," she says, interrupting me mid-thought. "The men do want you here."

A chill runs up my spine. "What are you saying?"

"I'm saying that I overheard a conversation." She pulls her lips in tight. "I heard Constance telling Jaison that she couldn't believe he made her invite you."

"Why the fuck?"

"I don't know, but something about that makes me uncomfortable. I know there are a lot of secrets amongst this group. Some of them, I know, and some, I don't want to know. Just watch yourself. Planning went into this weekend, and I don't think it was all just for the wedding."

As soon as she finishes that statement, the door slams open, and the rest of the women from our group file into the small space.

"Is this a girl's party, and we weren't invited?" Francesca asks in a syrupy sweet voice.

"Yeah," Constance says with a sneer. "This is supposed to be my celebration, my weekend." Her hands are on her hips as she leans toward us. It's obvious she's had more than just two flutes of champagne.

"Then, shouldn't you be with your husband?" I ask, unable to keep the barb from flying.

She calls me a bitch under her breath before Francesca announces that we're all going to the bar for drinks. I give my brightest smile before grabbing Tracy's arm as a lifeline. A boulder sits in the pit of my empty stomach.

six

ALESSANDRO

MY THOUGHTS ARE all over the place. On one hand, I want to stomp back into that room and pull her away. I want to put my hands everywhere they couldn't go right now. The feel of her skin has my body begging for more, and it was only that small sliver of her back. Shit, my cock is raging at me as much as my mind. I can't, however. I have to know what those assholes are planning and figure out how to stop it.

I hear them before I even enter the sports bar at the back of the casino. Their garish behavior pervades through even the noisiest areas of the ship. The group is huddled at a corner set of tables, empty shot glasses in front of them already. I shake my head and take a deep breath. After working my way through the crowd, I grab a chair near enough to hear their conversation without joining them. I'm tired of pretending to be a part of their group. It goes against every bit of goodness still left in me.

"When are the girls gonna join us?" Greg asks.

"I told my wife to go to the other bar and get a couple drinks in them first. We want this to be a party for everyone." The way Jaison says 'wife' is telling. He could've easily said her name, but he didn't. There might be something between him and the others that I can exploit.

"What're the odds Oddity agrees to do shots?" The calculating look on Arthur's face makes me want to punch him. I have no idea why the hell he's calling her that, but I know he's talking about Vette. He's only been that enthusiastically disgusting when talking about her or watching her.

"Dude, why does it matter?" Tony asks. Of all the men in the group, he's the only one who doesn't just go along with everything without questioning it. He wasn't even involved in the damage they did the last time we were on this ship. He had stayed at the bar when we all traveled below to the lower decks. I can't help but wonder what might have happened if he had come along. Maybe he could have talked some sense into Jaison and Arthur.

"Because, dipshit, she'll be less likely to run and hide if she's feeling good." Arthur rubs his hands together like a cartoon villain.

"Not that you mind the chase, eh Arthur," Jaison interjects with a knowing chuckle.

"I sure don't, but we've been playing cat and mouse since high school. It's time for her to give up the cat."

"What about Francesca?"

I wondered if someone was going to ask about Arthur's supposed relationship with one of the best friends. It seems that they've been together for a long time because I remember him talking about her five years ago.

"What about her, Tony?" Arthur answers with a shrug. "She knows the deal. She's mine, and as such, she gets all the benefit of my dick and my name, eventually. Only one of the two is exclusive."

"But I bet she doesn't get the benefit of being able to fuck around too," Greg says under his breath, and I chuckle.

"You're damn right, she doesn't. I don't want to be responsible for someone else's spawn. I'm not giving my name out to every damn body!"

Jaison snorts derisively, and I roll my eyes. A look passes between Tony and Greg, making me wonder if there isn't some secret they know that the others don't. I'm not sure what it might be, but I hope to find out because if I had my way about it, neither Jaison nor Arthur would have a damn name anymore. These guys need to be taken down a peg. The arrogance is unbelievable, and I can't wait to see it fade from their eyes.

An hour passes before the women join the group at the bar. Though they come in on a flurry of laughter, it is disingenuous. They're more reserved in their interactions with each other than I normally see with the guys. It's like they're putting on a show rather than collectively enjoying each other's company. Something feels off, but I can't put my finger on it. Then I look into Vette's eyes, and they're empty, as if she's here but not here at the same time. *What in the hell is going on?*

I wait until they join the table and look for an opportunity to get her attention. Constance, the bride, grabs a hold of her from the other woman whose name I'm not sure of, and there's a reluctance to release her that has my jaw working.

"Let me and Vette in," one of the women, I think Francesca, says to Arthur. "There's plenty of room on the bench for the two of us."

He stands immediately, situating himself behind Vette's beautiful frame, hands resting on her upper arms, but she doesn't shy away from him like she has before. She doesn't even say anything. He holds onto her while Francesca climbs into the booth and then he guides Vette onto the seat, pushing his way in next to her. In the meantime, Constance climbs across Tony. His hand rests a little too comfortably on her ass while he stabilizes her to get to Jaison's lap. They immediately start kissing, tongues down each other's throat, exhibition style while Tony watches them with a tight-lipped smile. The last woman whose name I still don't know sits next to Tony, her eyes never leaving Vette while Greg pulls up another chair.

I had been working out how to put my plans in motion, but the scene before me has me in knots. This cannot be good. From the moment I touched Vette's hand, I knew she would be a distraction I didn't need, but I can't pull myself away. I need to find a way to get close to her without garnering too much attention in the crowded bar.

"HOW'S IT feel to actually be part of the group, Oddity?" Arthur's question is a whisper in my ear. "You always try to stay on the outskirts rather than letting us get you out of that skirt. Let tonight be a lesson that you're not as smart as you think."

His voice penetrates the fog in my mind, but I can't respond. My body doesn't even react when he puts his hand on my thigh. What is happening to me? Why am I sitting next to Arthur? No, no, no, I can't be here. I shouldn't be here. Francesca's laughter comes from my other side. I know it's her because her voice is less shrill than Constance, though I hear her too.

"Look at her hanging out with us. If we had known that all it would take was a few strong drinks..." She said the word strong with a little too much emphasis.

I try blinking my eyes to brush away whatever it is that's holding me in place. The women laugh again, and I turn my head slightly. I can't quite focus on them, but I catch movement. A hand is slowly working its way up Francesca's thigh. That's Jaison's wedding ring. He's feeling up Francesca with Constance right here. I can hardly process that thought when Arthur begins caressing my thigh. His fingers squeeze, and his thumb makes circles on the outside of my thigh. The only clear thought in my head is to run, but I can't make myself move.

"Come on, Bella. Don't let them do this to you. Don't let them control you."

That voice. I know that voice. I don't feel the normal tingling sparks that happen whenever he's near, but I know his voice. I turn my head to look for him when I catch Tracy's eyes from across the table. Sadness and worry are written on her face as she chews her bottom lip. Someone is sitting next to her, but I can't focus on their face. And why can't I see or feel Alessandro if he's here? Why doesn't he do something to help me get out of this, to get me away from Arthur's grasp? Why doesn't anyone do something? Panic rises in my chest.

Arthur laughs, and the way his hand continues up my thigh has bile rising in my throat. I want to push him away, but my hands won't work right. I look at Tracy, silently pleading with her to help me, but then she's gone. Where did she go? My eyes move back and forth, and someone enters my field of vision, but I can't focus on them long enough to figure out how it is. I don't know how much time has passed before Tracy returns, her face resolute.

A few moments later, or maybe it's been minutes. An hour? I don't know. Finally, Arthur declares, "I gotta piss." In a whisper near my ear, he adds, "Don't go nowhere. I have plans for you." With a quick squeeze of my thigh, he's gone.

"Now, Bella. Now is the time to get out of here. You can do it." The voice echoes through my mind, but I still don't see him. I can't find him.

Tracy stands. "I think I'm gonna get some fresh air. Vette, why don't you join me?" My head flops forward, and I hope it looks like a nod. I can't do much more than that.

"We're supposed to be celebrating our wedding," Constance whines.

"Stop upsetting my wife, and chill out." Jaison's voice doesn't have its normal scathing tone.

"We're just going to get some fresh air and then come back in," Tracy says, reaching down to take my arm and help me up.

"I'll go with them and make sure they make it back," Tony offers.

"Fine," Jaison says, his voice resigned.

"Arthur's going to be pissed," Francesca adds, her voice breathier than normal.

My eyes look to where I was just sitting, and Jaison's hand is all the way up Francesca's skirt. Either Constance doesn't notice, or she doesn't care. I can't bring myself to care. If he's busy with her, he doesn't seem to care about me, and I need to get out of here before Arthur comes back. Using what little control I have, I turn my head and shoot imploring eyes at Tracy.

"Come on, girl, let's go for a walk," she says aloud for everyone to hear. She follows it with, "We need to get you out of here," under her breath.

She helps me slide to the end of the bench where Tony takes over, lifting me to a standing position and putting his arm around my waist. She then grabs my arm from the other side. I look up, and Alessandro is standing by the door of the bar. It looks like he's beckoning me to come that way. Why isn't he here helping me? Why didn't he step in earlier? He has to see how out of it I am, and why isn't he with the group? My brain is so fuzzy.

"I can't stay outside for long, Tracy. Arthur's going to beat my ass for taking her out of there."

"Do you think that's worse than what he's planning to do to her in the state she's in?"

"I'm here helping, aren't I? This whole situation is fucked up! Every damn time, they have to get into some shit."

"What do you mean every time?"

"Nevermind."

They continue walking, or rather dragging, me through the ships and we just make it into the elevator when I hear Arthur's voice bellow.

"I don't even understand what the four of them are doing or why we're even here with them," Tracy continues railing. Things were fun when we were in high school. They were cool in college, but this shit..." she trails off.

"Yeah," he agrees. "This shit isn't cool. They're not all the same, though." He continues after a moment. "Constance isn't really like the others."

Something that resembles a snort leaves me. I would've laughed out loud at his statement had I had full control of my faculties, but only that sound made an escape. Hopefully, that means whatever is in my system is making its way out.

"Vette, are you okay? Can you talk now?" I look up at her and am able to shake my head slightly. "What in the world did they give you? How in the hell did they get it is another question. And why did they agree to it?" Tracy continues her litany of questions, trying to work out details that really aren't important right now. The important thing is getting me to safety away from everyone. "Girl, I wish you had told us where your room was. These damn key cards don't have room numbers on them, and the staff isn't going to help." She hardly takes a breath before continuing. "It's not safe for me to take you to my room. Everyone knows where that is."

"Figure out something, Trace. I have to go back soon, and I have to have something to tell them. If they're willing to do this to her, who knows what else they're willing to do."

"Well, we just can't leave her somewhere, Tony. Could we

maybe ask someone to take her to her room even if they won't tell us where it is?"

"That might work," he responds in a contemplative tone.

My head reels. They're going to ask a random person, a random stranger, to take me to my room. They're actually going to leave me alone with someone else and trust them to take me to my room. I am in some kind of fucking nightmare right now, and I can't wake up from it.

"Hey, do you have one of those machines that can tell you what room someone is in," Tony asks.

I don't know who he's talking to, but I hear them respond with uncertainty. "Yes, but I'm unable to tell you any information about another guest who isn't in your room."

"I understand that," Tony says with exasperation, "but my friend here has had far too much to drink, and she never told us what her room number was. For her safety and our sanity, she needs to get back to her room."

"Sir, I can't tell you what her room number is even if I scan her card. Unless she is in the room with you or is in a room that is connected to your party, I can't tell you the number."

"We understand that," Tracy says. Her tone is appeasing, and my heart breaks. They are really trying to give me away to someone. "Can you scan it and help her to the room?"

They man they're talking to hesitates, and my stomach ties in knots. I want to go to my room and hide. I don't, however, want to be left alone with some unknown man, even if he does work here on the ship.

"Well, she does look incapacitated. Is she even able to walk?"

"You have to hold her stable, but yes, her legs work. She will walk with you." Tony's answer is quick.

"Maybe we should take her to the infirmary."

"No, no, she just needs to sleep it off." I can hear the panic in Tony's voice.

Yes, yes, take me to the infirmary, I scream in my head. Please take me to the infirmary. Find out what the hell it is that they gave me.

"This isn't the first time she's had too much to drink."

What is he saying? I've never gotten drunk around them ever. A noise of exasperation leaves me, but still I can't get out any words. I will my hands to grasp Taylor's arm, to do something.

"Fine. Let me scan her card." A hand lifts the lanyard hanging around my neck, and I hear a beep. "It's on a different floor, but I will take her."

"Thank you," Tracy says, and I hear relief in her voice.

"You take care of her," Tony says as two sets of hands relinquish me to another.

The man wraps one arm around my waist and puts my arm around his neck.

"Come on, let's get you into the elevator."

A tear rolls down my cheek. I've gone from one dangerous situation to another. All these years that I've done so well protecting myself from them...

"You sure are pretty," the man says while we stand in front of the elevator.

I still haven't seen his face clearly yet. Each time I've turned my head to look at him, he's been in profile or looking away. If only I could look into his eyes, maybe I could read his intent. Maybe he'd feel sorry for me and take me to the doctor.

"This is a lovely dress you have on."

My stomach tightens. Those are not the words of a man who will be my savior.

"Let's get you downstairs," he says, and his hand tightens on my waist.

There has to be some way of stopping this. I will my legs to lock, but nothing happens. I will my arms to swing, but nothing happens. He practically carries me into the elevator, and when the door slides shut, I close my eyes.

"You can't even talk, can you? I wonder how much of this you'll remember in the morning. What were your friends thinking just leaving you alone with someone none of you know? Is that how friends are?"

He may be asking questions, but they're obviously rhetorical. Each one sets off a tendril of fear. The man is deranged.

"No. Friends take care of you. Do you want me to take care of you?"

Bile rises in my throat. They should've just left me with Arthur. If I'm going to be raped anyway, it might as well be by someone I know. Someone I know who's wanted to fuck me for years. Someone who won't do anything worse for fear of the repercussions since I know who he is and my family knows who he is.

The man turns me toward him, and I get a glance of his face before I'm pulled against his chest. He sniffs my hair, and his hand reaches down to grab my ass.

"You're so soft, like a juicy peach. I bet you'll drip all over me." He squeezes my ass cheek harder, and I'm sure that if I survive this, there will be a massive bruise for days. "You would think," he says, continuing his rumination, "that with all these people on the ship, and all of us who work here, we would never get lonely. That's not the case, though. It can get very lonely." His keys jingle. "How about you and I spend some time alone together and relieve some of this loneliness. Most people won't use the elevator right now anyway, at least not until shift change. I'll lock it just in case to give us some privacy."

The man leans me against the elevator wall to focus on

putting his key in the slot, and I hear Alessandro's voice. I hear him, and tears fall from my eyes because there's no way he can be here. I'm stuck in this elevator alone with a man who intends to rape me.

"I'm here with you, Bella. Take my hand and let me hold you."

A sob escapes my lips, and the man turns to look at me. I feel the staticky tingles spread from my shoulder, down my arm, and to my hand as fingers interlock with mine. The man turns back toward me, and his eyes grow wide. I no sooner see his mouth fall open, then I am pulled away from the elevator wall and wrapped in strong arms. The elevator begins to shake, and strange noises come from the man behind me. I burrow my face into Alessandro's chest, letting out tears of fear, frustration, and anger.

"Shhh my beautiful, Odveta. You did so well. Just hold on to me, and it will all be over soon."

Where did he come from? How does he know my real name? I have so many questions, but none of them process once the smell of charred flesh reaches my nostrils. I let out a whimper.

"We will talk about everything once I get you safely back to your room. I'm so glad you let me accompany you earlier, else I wouldn't know where to go."

The elevator door opens, and he ushers me out into the fresher air of an empty hall. I don't even try to look behind us for the other man. Nothing matters except staying cocooned in the safety of Alessandro's arms.

ALESSANDRO

WE GET TO HER ROOM, and I manage to open the door with her keycard. I want to put her somewhere safe, somewhere comfortable. Anger at what they've done to her courses through me. My first thought is to lay her on the bed, but my thoughts go sideways. That is not what she needs right now. I want to make sure the door is secured, so I lean her against the wall and step back.

"Don't leave me...please."

They're the first words I've heard her say in hours, and I turn to look in her eyes. They're big as saucers, full of fear and something else I can't quite read. Still, her coherence quells my emotions.

"I just want to make sure the door closes. I'm not going anywhere."

She lets out a breath of relief. I take two steps from her and reach for the handle. *Shit! How?* I rub my hand down my face. I just opened the door a minute ago. How do I make this happen? The door may be closed all the way, but the lock isn't fully engaged. A steward can still come in.

"Bella, I need your help," I say with a sigh. She still hasn't moved, which means the drug they gave her is still working through her system. This is going to sound strange, but we can talk about it when you are fully back to yourself."

"Ok...I guess." Her forehead scrunches.

"We're going to take a couple steps toward the door. I need to test something."

"Test?"

"I promise to explain." I look at her, my eyes as soft as I can make them. I don't know how I'm going to make her understand, but I'll do whatever it takes. I place my hand on her cheek. "So much has happened in such a short period of time, but the only thing that matters right now is you."

That is the truth, my truth. The moment the words have left my mouth, I know them to be true. If she told me to, I would throw all of my plans away and plan for nothing else but her. First, though, we need to get that door locked. I bring her closer, close enough that I can keep our hands clasped together and reach the lock. I've watched the zing of electricity go through her a number of times today, and I can't get enough of the sight. Her touch affects me differently, but to see her taken with mine is something I've never imagined. I reach out and grab the latch, trying to turn the lock, but it doesn't go. My brows draw together.

"Is something wrong?"

"No, everything's fine," I lie. "The lock just seems to be stuck."

"And you needed me over here to help you unstick the lock?"

"I needed you close. I feel better, more whole...more like myself when I'm near you, when I'm touching you." I look into her eyes when I say the last part. I need her to know it's not a lie. She makes me whole and somehow has turned the whole world topsy-turvy in little more than twelve hours. "Now, I need this damn door to lock," I say. I turn my frustration and anger at tonight's events on the wooden plank and slam my fist against it. A loud thud resounds through the room, and an audible gasp leaves Vette's mouth.

"Sorry, Bella." I reach out and turn the lock. It slides into place smoothly.

"I understand your frustration," she says. "I have been feeling frustrated most of the evening.

"I know. I wish I could have kept that from you."

"I have so many questions. Why weren't you there? When you were there, why didn't you help? Why were you so far away from the group? I could hear your voice, but I couldn't see you sometimes."

"I know, I know," I say and kiss her forehead. "I will answer all your questions as best I can once you're well. I don't know what they did to you, but I saw that empty look in your eye, and it shattered me. They will regret it! But first, we need to wait out the effects. Then we talk. Trust me." I cup her cheek. I want to kiss those lips, but I don't. Instead, I lead her to the bed, pull down the covers, and tuck her in.

"You're not leaving me, are you?"

"Get some rest. I'll be right here when you wake up."

I wait until she is fully asleep before I pass through the door and make my way back to the bar. I doubt they're still there, but I will find them. If I have to scour every inch of this ship, I will find them.

nine

ALESSANDRO

AS I THOUGHT, the group is no longer in the sports bar. They haven't stopped drinking, however. I find two of them in the casino, drinks in front of them.

"Are you alright, Trace? You haven't quite been the same since after the cocktail hour, and you've gotten progressively distant since you and Tony returned without Vette."

"Yeah, Greg. I'm fine. I'm just worried about Vette and hope she'll be feeling better in the morning." She goes quiet for a few seconds before adding. "I didn't like leaving her, but I also didn't want to hear Constance and Francesca complain if I didn't come back to the party. They can be real bitches sometimes. Selfish as fuck!"

"You're not wrong about that. It seems they found the perfect men." He looks around, like one of their friends might pop up behind them at any second. "I'm honestly surprised they haven't all moved in together since they just keep swinging back and forth," he says with a chuckle.

"Stop," she says, slapping his shoulder, a smile on her face.

"You know it's true. Jaison would probably gladly fuck both of them at the same time, and though Arthur wouldn't want to admit it, he'd do the same thing. He just wouldn't want Francesca to get any pleasure from it. Now that's a selfish bastard. The friends we keep, huh?" he says with a snort, and they both go back to the games they were playing.

These two were never in the plan, and if nothing changes, they might be left alone. I'm still not happy that Tracy left Vette alone with that charcoal briquette downstairs in the elevator, but I can understand her reluctance to let anyone in the group down.

I find Tony and Constance at the rear of the ship with their feet in the hot tub. Neither of them have changed their clothes. They're just sitting there.

"I can't believe Jaison left you alone on your wedding night."

"He'll come back and find me. He won't stay gone for long. He was just worried about the kind of trouble Arthur would get himself into trying to find the damn Oddity." She shakes her head with a sneer. "I should've never invited her, should've never let my parents talk me into it. It's not like she really wanted to come anyway. Her parents made a big stink about it as well. For some reason, the old folks seem to think that we've been this great friend group since forever. No. We've just been together because of them. I'd have gotten rid of her a long time ago."

"Don't talk like that! You sound like Jaison and Arthur when you talk like that, and you're better than that."

"I like that you think that of me," she says, placing a kiss on his cheek.

"Did you really have to marry him?"

Before she turns back to him, she wrinkles her nose and rolls her eyes. "We've already talked about this, Tony. My family needs the connection."

"And what about what you need?"

"I need the freedom to be able to do what I want," she says, placing her hand on his knee.

"And where does that leave me, C?"

"What do you mean? You're one of the things I want to do?"

He pulls away from her and stands. "So I'm just one of your things, huh?" He turns away from her and walks toward the bar.

"Tony, come back," she whines, but he doesn't turn around.

Good for him. Hopefully, he's learned a lesson. That doesn't make up for the situation he put Vette into tonight, but I can tell where his heart is, or at least where it was. Love is a funny thing.

My thoughts fly back to the woman I left alone in bed. I won't be so presumptuous as to say love is in the cards for us, but there's definitely a spark of something. I leave Constance sitting there pouting. She never even notices my presence. It's so quiet back here right now, it would be easy to reach out and push her into the hot tub and hold her head under the water. My fingers twitch at the idea, but while my plans have changed slightly, there is an order to things. It's not time yet, and she is not the first on my list. I have to find the two who have haunted my dreams for five fucking years.

They're not on either of the two main decks, nor do I notice Francesca. After the conversation between Greg and Tracy, I wonder if they aren't all back in a room together. Then, I catch a glimpse of golden-boy hair. At this time of night, when most people have gone off to bed or are inside at the dance clubs, it's not hard to find a 6-foot-three playboy with golden blonde hair. Arthur wanders, almost aimlessly, but having watched him before, I can tell he's a man on a mission. His head sweeps back and forth searching, and his gait is purposeful.

"Where the fuck is she?" he asks aloud to no one. "She didn't just fucking disappear. She couldn't even walk on her own. I could fucking kill Tony right now, spoiling all my fun for the night. She was supposed to be my gift for the fucking weekend, for agreeing to this return to Spirit." I smile at the irony as he continues to ramble to himself aloud. "I never wanted to come back on this ship. Who the fuck would want to return to this place? We were lucky to get out of here the first time." He trails off, putting his hands on the window beside him. He appears to scan the workout room and then shakes his head with a chuckle. "Her fat ass wouldn't be in here, even if she wasn't drugged."

He shakes his head and continues walking. I have the urge to tackle him to the ground and bash his face in for the way he talks about Vette. Every curve of her body is perfect. Her skin is just as soft to the touch as the rest of her. I am going to enjoy carrying out my play time with him the most, I think as I continue following him around the front of the ship.

Arthur doesn't seem to notice, but I hear a familiar female laugh on the wind. When we get to the stairs that lead to the adults-only section of the ship, I watch him walk off, grateful that Vette is safely asleep in her room. His preoccupation with her telling me that everyone else on the ship is likely safe as well...well, except for Tony. He can take one for the team, I decide with a chuckle and start my climb to the serenity deck, the voices direct me to the alcove where a lone covered daybed sits.

These things are big enough for four people, and the staff hates to clean them. There's no doubt that multiple people use them for sexual rendezvous. Truth be told, they are a great place for a public tryst where you're unlikely to get caught if you can stay quiet. Jaison and Francesca, however, don't care about staying quiet. Her moans float across the air along with his growls of pleasure.

"You taste so fucking good. You've been wet as fuck all

night, haven't you? You're so naughty. You loved me playing with your pussy while Constance was sitting on my lap." Francesca giggles. "I wonder if Arthur knows how naughty you are."

There's a sudden slap, and I hear her gasp. Then slurping noises begin from behind the cover. I don't need to look to know what is happening. I'm of the mind to lead Arthur back this way though. We don't often get to see fireworks from the ship, but I'm sure there would be fireworks if he caught them together. I shake my head and head back to Vette's room. I've left her alone long enough, and I want to keep my promise of being there when she wakes.

ten

ALESSANDRO

VETTE'S CURLED into a ball when I enter the room, and she's thrown the covers off like she'd gotten overheated in her sleep. Her back is toward the door, and her thick thighs are on display. I'm immediately hard at the view and press down on the bulge in my pants trying to control the desire that rushes through me. She is fucking perfect! The dress is pulled up slightly, cupping just under her ass. If it were any higher, I'd see her panties, which is not a thought I need when I'm trying to relieve an erection, but I can't help it. The curves of her body call to be touched, and that gold dress complements her skin tone perfectly. The peep of her bare back is sensual without being vulgar, and her hair hangs loosely from the messy bun she'd put it in earlier. It's splayed out over the bed, and I want to wrap my fingers in it.

I sit in the chair against the wall, just watching her with my legs stretched out in front of me, one ankle crossed over the other. At this moment, the only place I'd rather be is cuddled against her, but she's asleep. After all she's been through tonight, I won't do that to her. I won't be the one to take advantage of her. At some point, she shifts her body and a shiver courses over her. She reaches out a hand as if she's trying to find the blanket, but then she says my name.

"Alessandro, where are you?"

"I'm right here, Bella."

She stretches out her hand and turns her head toward my voice. Her eyes, however, are still closed. She must be dreaming. I smile at the idea of her dreaming about me. Suddenly, she sits up, and I pull my legs back until my feet are flat on the floor, ready to jump to whatever need she might have.

"What do you need, Vette?"

I don't expect her to answer, as I'm sure she's still sleeping. I'm not sure if she walks or talks in her sleep normally, or if this is possibly the effects of coming down from the drug. It's hard to tell when I haven't been able to figure out what it was they had given her.

"It's hot in here. Why's it so hot in here?"

She reaches down and pulls the hem of the dress up. My mouth drops when she then pulls at the front of her dress. A groan escapes her before she reaches to unbutton the clasp behind her neck, exposing her back. I hadn't noticed earlier, but there is one thin strap going around her lower back and one clear strap around her neck. Presumably, they are what's holding her bra on. My mouth waters with the urge to taste her skin. I want to run my tongue up her spine. I tell myself I should stop this, should stop her, or that I should leave, but I'm frozen in place.

Her hands slide down, uncovering the swell of her breasts in the plunge bra she's wearing. How that thing is holding her in place, I don't know. For the amount of coverage it provides, she might as well be naked. Every part of me wishes she were naked. Again, I tell myself to leave, but that voice inside me says she asked for me to stay, so here I sit. She runs her hands up her thighs, pushing the hem of the dress up until I can see the entirety of her hip that leads to the roundness of her ass where she sits. The bottom of the dress still hugs her firmly, though the top is loose and hanging down around her waist. At this point, there is little covering her, and she is glorious.

I can tell her golden skin is natural. There is not one line on her, but I can see every dimple, every roll that I just want to grab a hold of to take a bite. There's no doubt she will taste as delicious as she looks right now. Still that voice of doubt kicks in wondering if I'd actually be able to taste her. She may bring my senses to life, but is it all of them? That question in my mind and the sound of my name on her lips take away all further thought. I take two steps toward the bed and climb behind her, pressing my chest against her back.

Vette lays her head back against my chest, her right hand coming up to slide around my neck pulling me closer. My hands find their way to her waist, and I circle it. Her breasts are a hands' width away from my fingertips, teasing me with their fullness. Releasing my neck, she yanks the strap over her head. My breaths grow heavy and hers quicken. Again, she grabs my head and turns hers to the side, giving me full access to her neck. I groan before placing a soft kiss where her neck and shoulder meet. I bite my bottom lip and give her another kiss, my mouth slightly open. Nerves and desire war within me, but her fingers in my hair, and the gentle tug as she tightens her grip pushing nerves aside.

I run my tongue up the length of her neck. The saltiness of her skin mixed with the tangy sweetness of whatever perfume she'd put on earlier drag a moan from me that can probably be heard throughout the ship. I gently nip at her earlobe, and she whimpers. My hand slides up, grabbing the fabric of her plunge bra that is just there in the way and pulling it down, releasing her tits. I cup them, and they overflow my hands, perfectly weighted.

"You are so perfect," I whisper against her ear. "Lay back and let me taste you."

She turns her head toward me, and I capture her lips before she can say anything, before I can think twice. Her mouth is hot and wet. There's no minty freshness, no pretense. The taste of her realness turns me on even more. I can't imagine a woman as put together as her lets many taste her rawness. I devour her like the starved man I am without any gentleness, knowing her lips will be swollen by the time we're done. I need her. I need her more than breath, more than air or food. At this moment, I just need to taste her.

The electrical charge between us hums, and my cock awakens fully, screaming like Frankenstein's monster. I've gotten hard over the past few years. Hell, I've been hard almost every time I've stood near her or looked at her or heard her voice throughout the past twenty hours. I can't believe it hasn't even been a full day, yet I'm consumed by her. I want to consume her and keep her with me. When a small yelp and moan leave her mouth, I realize I'm not only kneading her breasts but also pinching and twisting her nipples. My tongue continues to dance with hers. I pull away, nibbling on her lips, my teeth and tongue finding their way to her jaw. My hands find the final clasp on her bra and fling it to the floor.

"Lay down," I tell her, and she does.

I make quick work of removing the dress that no longer covers anything except the small strip around her middle. I want to see all of her laid out before me. When she's left in nothing more than a pair of panties, black lace with gold threads to match the gold in her dress, I take a deep breath, soaking in the portrait that she paints against the white sheets of the bed. Her hair is a tangle of curls around her head in a dark halo. She is my dark angel.

"Tell me, Angel," I say, leaning over her, a hair's breadth between our lips, "what does Odveta mean?"

She smiles and brings her lips to mine before she pulls my bottom lip into her mouth, her teeth biting down just enough to make me moan. My hand cups her cheek until I slide it up into her hair, grabbing a handful and pulling. Her eyes sparkle and the moan she releases touches my lips. I lay my cheek against hers, my lips near her ear. "Tell me, please." She runs her tongue up the outer ridge of my ear, and I shudder, completely bewitched by this woman. In this moment, she is both my undoing and my creator, as nothing else exists but her.

"Vengeance," she says against my ear.

A sound I don't think I've ever made before, something like a growl, leaves my throat. "And vengeance is mine," I say, my voice raspy, as I make my way down her body, pulling her perfect nipples into my mouth and running my teeth across each tight bud. She moans, and it's a symphony in my head, a soundtrack that is both soothing and empowering. Every plan I have put in place, every careful thought I've had over the past five years, morphs, melting and reforming until everything is clear. There is nothing but the shape, the smell, the touch of her, my vengeance made flesh.

My mouth descends on her pussy, my tongue sliding into her slit for the first taste. A crackle of electricity buzzes around us. With my hands holding her open to me, I devour her. Our moans combine into an explosion that just might tip the ship, and I can't bring myself to care. She's on my tongue, coating my lips, drenching me in her release, and yet, I want more. I slip my tongue inside her, feasting on every drop. She screams my name, and I'm alive for the first time.

CHAPTER 11

eleven

VETTE

I'VE NEVER FELT anything like Alessandro's mouth. It is both heaven and torture at the same time. Those tiny sparks I always feel when he touches me are now a flame. Every inch of my body is on fire. I don't know how or when it started, but I'm a mass of kindling, and his tongue fans the flame.

"Don't stop," I cry out, reaching down to fist my hand in his hair. He looks up, his tongue flat against my clit, and I nearly explode at the desire, the need, and the ecstasy in his eyes when they lock on mine. I've never had a man look at me that way before. I moan as waves of pleasure flow through me, his name pulled from me like a prayer. My release is hard and swift, all-encompassing, but he doesn't stop. His tongue plunges into me as he nips, licks, and sucks every inch of my pussy. My clit throbs, swollen and aching for him. What should be satisfaction is just a tantalizing need. My entire body is buzzing, charged with this connection between us. It's like every want, every desire, every need I've ever felt is made flesh in this man. When he declared I was his, I thought it was just a quirky play on my name, but it was the truth manifested. I am his. There's no part of me that doesn't call out, reach out for him.

My voice is huskier than I've ever heard it when I say, "Make me yours."

He sits up, his hands on his knees, looking down on me like he's worshiping a goddess. The look says he can't believe I'm here laid out before him. He pulls his shirt over his head, not bothering to unbutton it. His chest is firm muscle, his skin a tawny beige like it yearns for the sun's touch. My eyes trail down to where his hands sit on his belt buckle. I know he's watching me take him in, and I bite my bottom lip in anticipation. He is slow and methodical, pulling the belt from the loops and tossing it in the same direction as his shirt, possibly the same direction as my dress. I have no idea when that left my body.

He unbuttons his pants, and my eyes are caught on the line of dark hair trailing from his navel to right inside his waistband. I go to sit up, to reach for him, but he shakes his head and stands from the bed before letting his pants fall. His cock springs free, and a breath, a simple puff of air leaves my lips as my mouth waters at the sight of it. The sight of him standing there is glorious. His body has sinewy muscles from top to bottom. I want to taste him, to have every inch of him in my mouth, his lips saying my name. Before he can protest, I flip onto my stomach. My hand grabs his shaft, pulling him to my open mouth. I run the tip of my tongue around the head, and he moans. I don't know that I've ever heard a more delicious sound.

I take him into my mouth, working the length with my hand until I can swallow the entire thing. Our moans intermingle, and he fists my hair, holding me in place until my eyes water. My pussy throbs with the need to be filled like my throat. He rocks his hips, and I flatten my tongue, giving him space to give us both pleasure.

His praise and sounds of pleasure nearly have me falling

apart again, but I want him inside of me. I want to be his completely. Never have I felt a need so strong before. Now, I could blame it on my self-imposed dry spell, but that's not it. There is something about this man that speaks to my soul. Pulling him from my mouth with a pop, I smile up at him, kissing my way up his torso, running my tongue through the ridges of his muscles. I want to trace them in my memory. Our eyes never leave each other. His are hungry, pupils dilated, and my body responds, arching toward him.

The boat rocks, and I look toward the balcony window. We've sailed into a storm. Somehow, the torrent outside feeds the fire we've stoked inside. When I am up, even with his lips, we stay there, staring into each other's eyes, breaths intermingling. Moments pass before I manage to say the words that push us over the edge.

"Take your vengeance."

He pushes me back and then wraps his hands around my thighs, pulling me to the edge of the bed. "My vengeance is not gentle."

"Fuck me," I say, my voice husky, as the force of his words and the honesty of them in his eyes have me nearly undone.

His hands find my breasts, massaging the peaks until they're hard and pebbled again, sending short currents through my body straight to my core. He leans over, my legs on his shoulders until my knees touch my chest, and takes each of the nipples into his mouth. He lines the tip of his cock against my entrance, but he's taking too long. I use the strength of his shoulders to leverage my legs, lifting my hips until I feel him stretching me open.

"Shit," I moan, stretching out the single syllable.

This is the sweetest torture. He lifts his head and looks at me one more time before raising up and driving his hips forward. A scream exits my lips, more from surprise than pain, though he has me stretched in a way I haven't been for a long time. He stays there for a few moments until my hips start circling of their own accord, my core seeking out the friction his intrusion promised. He growls low in his throat, and I bite my lower lip, trying to hide the smile when he pulls his hips back. I whimper when just the head remains inside me.

His breathing is heavy like he's trying to hold back. I don't want him to hold back. I reach down toward where we're joined and try to grab for his shaft. He grabs my hand instead and holds my fingers to my swollen clit, pulling a moan from me at the sensation.

"Touch yourself for me, sweet vengeance."

I start rubbing circles over the sensitive nub. He pushes back inside of me all the way, working himself in and out in small movements. My mouth drops open as ecstasy invades my senses. His moans mingle with mine, and I meet him thrust for thrust.

"Come for me, Odveta. Take me with you."

His words are less a command and more a plea, so I speed up my movements to meet his request. My body tenses the moment before I explode, and when he screams his release, electricity flows through me. The lights in the room flicker and screams come from the hallway. We stare into each other's eyes as our heartbeats wane in sync. He holds his mouth tightly together while I suck in both of my lips until we both burst out laughing.

"Well, that was..." I pause to think of the right word.

"Shocking," he offers.

"That's one way of putting it," I say, and we fall into fits of laughter again when the lights come back on in the room. "Do you think we should check and make sure no permanent damage was done anywhere?"

"They'll be fine," he says, his face stoic. "Ships are often hit by lightning, and rarely does anyone notice."

I open my mouth and close it a few times, a question forming in the back of my mind. He cups my face.

"I see you thinking, but let's get you cleaned up first." He looks down at himself, sweat still evident on his torso and the mixture of our releases proof of our shared experience. "Let's get us cleaned up," he corrects.

I laugh again. I haven't been this comfortable and relaxed with a man in years. Last night went so wrong, but this morning...this morning has been utter perfection.

"What if we ordered room service and never left this room for the rest of the cruise?" I ask before I can think better of it.

He turns toward me with a glint in his eye, but there's also something else, something almost sad in that look. Without a word, he reaches out a hand and I get up from the bed. I don't know what he thinks we're going to do together. The showers are not the right size for two full-grown adults, and I'm a little thicker than most.

"We're not gonna fit in the shower together," I tell him as he pulls me into the tiny bathroom.

"We are, and we will. If everything gets soaked, we are on a ship. It'll be fine."

I can't help but laugh at his deadpan face when he says something that seems so nonsensical. At the same time, it gets me back to thinking of the question that stuck in my mind earlier.

"What did I tell you?" He says. "Clean first, then think."

He turns his hand behind my neck and pulls my lips to his. All thinking ceases. All I can do is feel as he pushes me back against the wall, his mouth greedily devouring mine again. While his hands slip down my body, now slick from the spray, I brace myself on the safety bar, my hips placed precariously along its length when his hands trail lower.

"Don't think. Don't talk. Just feel," he says, his voice gruff and demanding.

I nod my head as words elude me. His hand massages my nipple, and his mouth makes its way from my neck to my lips. When his tongue touches mine, he plunges two fingers inside of me. A whimper escapes, and then I'm riding his hand, the heel of his palm rubbing against my clit. The friction is exactly what my body needs to fall over the edge. When the orgasm pulses through my body, it's his name on my lips, and I know the feel of him will haunt me forever.

twelve

ALESSANDRO

LYING HERE WITH VETTE, it's easy to let the rest of the world just fade away. After these past few years, I don't know whether I believe in heaven anymore, but her soft breaths, her plush body, and the peaceful feeling that's come over me are about as close to heaven as I had ever imagined. Morning light streams through the window, and I brush a wisp of hair off her face. I want to stay like this forever and let out a long sigh at the conversation that I know will come all too soon.

Loud talking outside the door and the sound of a vacuum cleaner down the hall bring me back to reality, a reality in which all of this is temporary. This feeling, her in my arms, the passing hours before the ship docks at its home port...it's all temporary. A pit forms in the base of my stomach. When she stirs slightly, I pull her closer, not wanting to let it all end just yet. And when she opens her eyes, still unfocused from the satiated sleep she had been enjoying, I kiss her soft lips. Immediately, she pulls back as if stung by the jolt of electricity that had driven us last night. She stares at me wide-eyed and looks around the room. I don't say a word. Nothing can take away this initial shock.

"Shit! What are you doing here? How did I get back here? What the fuck happened?" With each question, her voice rises and so does she until she's looking at me from a seated position. "Are you just going to sit there and stare at me?"

She's beautiful still, even in this space between disbelief and anger. With streams of sunlight haloing around her dark hair, she is truly a goddess.

"I will try to answer all your questions as best I can. As to why I'm here..." I shrug. "I couldn't stay away." I give her a wan smile. "Something drew me to you from the moment I saw you across the chapel room, and I couldn't keep my distance. After what happened last night, I couldn't leave you alone. I needed to know you were safe."

"What happened last night?" she asks, panic leaking into her voice. Why were you worried for my safety? And why the fuck are you in my bed?"

Those are all good and legitimate questions. I lift my hands in a placating gesture. She has every reason to be freaking out, and that feeling is only going to grow as I answer her questions.

"Last night, a couple of your friends..." I say the last word with a sneer. "slipped something into your drink. It incapacitated you to the point you were like a zombie. Tracy, I believe it is, and one of the guys got you out of the bar, but they didn't know your room number, so they left you in the bowels of the ship with someone who works here." I shake my head. "Correction, someone who no longer works at all." Her brows draw together, but I'm not ready to have that part of the conversation yet. "I found you with him in the elevator and brought you back to the room. I tucked you into bed fully dressed and sat there in that chair." I pointed at the lone armchair against the wall.

"You brought me back here?"

There's such sadness in that question, as if she just now

realized how vulnerable she was last night. I wait while her mind processes everything I've told her thus far. After several moments, she laughs derisively.

"I knew they were capable of some shady shit, but to drug me... What the fuck? Why?"

"I don't know for certain, but I have a feeling it was for Arthur. I overheard him say something about you being his gift for this weekend." I can hardly get the words out without snarling, the urge to find them all right now and make them pay nearly taking over, but the look in her eyes holds me in place.

"I knew I should've never agreed to this weekend," she says quietly. "Arthur and Jaison have been trying to get in my pants since high school. I don't even know why. Neither of them like me. They never have. I was the fat girl with the odd name, and yet every chance they could get to find me alone or corner me, they would. I should've known better. I should've told my parents no, that I wouldn't subject myself to whatever games they had planned. But you, what are you doing with them? You aren't part of our social circle. Why are you with them, in addition to being naked in my bed? I can assume the answer to that."

"You'd only be partially right in your assumption, Bella." She scoffs, and I take a deep breath. "I met the guys the last time they were on this ship." Her head tilts to the side with a questioning look, but she doesn't say anything to interrupt. "It was five years ago, and I worked here. It can get pretty boring when you work on a ship. All the passengers come for the entertainment but walk past without actually seeing us unless they need something. When we're not on the clock, we usually stay below deck, not even getting a chance to enjoy the luxuries ourselves." I want to pause there, but I know if I don't push through, it will only get harder to tell her everything.

"So, I was working at the bar one night and met this

gregarious group of guys. They seemed to be having a lot of fun, and they actually talked to me. They used my name, and invited me to sit with them though I was still working. It was a great night." I give her a smile to punctuate the truth of my statement. I had a wonderful time that first night. "The next day, I found as many excuses as I could to find them on the ship and hang out with them. I should've known better," I say, mirroring her earlier statement. "I'd seen so many groups like them, but most of those people just ignored me. There was something about feeling included in the fun after so many months at sea."

She sits quietly, hands folded in her lap. I can't read her expression, but at least she's not running from me...yet. My body tenses with the understanding that she will be soon.

"Anyway, that second night, they asked about secret places those of us who work here hang out. I guess for them, it was kind of like 'how do the ordinary people live' or something like that. I told them about the different alcoves and rooms where we would play cards sometimes, and Jaison asked me to show them. I knew we weren't supposed to take anyone down there, but my new friends asked, so I showed them the way."

She shakes her head in a combination of disappointment and resignation that I feel to my bones. We're kindred in our relationship with this crew of miscreants, and yet, I'm embarrassed to tell her what my poor decision caused.

<h1>thirteen</h1>

ALESSANDRO

THERE'S tension in the air. Odveta sits wringing her hands, waiting for me to continue my story. I want to reach out and grab her hands but think better of it. The only way to save her from this truth is to disappear from her sight completely, and I can't do that. I can't be without her. She is my lifeline. After several deep breaths, I let the rest of the story flow.

"While we were down there chilling and drinking, a member of the cleaning staff came by. She was new, quiet, and too damn good to be around them. They invited her to have a drink. She was too afraid to say no. I was too afraid to force her to say no. I figured one drink, if she agreed to it, couldn't hurt. I was wrong."

I closed my eyes tightly against the memory, and Vette grabbed my hand in hers. I let out a long breath.

"After that one drink, she left. I didn't know that Arthur followed her until a while later when I realized he'd been gone from the room. Jaison swore Arthur went to the bathroom, so I went to make sure he hadn't gotten lost. He was in the middle of raping that girl. There was blood everywhere. He had slapped her around, and she was lying limp while he pounded in and out of her."

Vette gasps, and I squeeze her hand, but I don't stop the story. I can't. I'll never be able to get started again.

"I couldn't believe what I was seeing. Guilt, anger, anguish. I felt them all at the same time. I was also afraid of what would happen to me for having brought them down there. I didn't think. I just jumped in, wrestling him off of her, screaming at him about 'What the fuck was wrong with him.' He laughed in response. He was covered in her blood, and he laughed. I wanted to kill him at that moment."

I take a few deep breaths, trying to calm the adrenaline building with the memories. Vette's hands on mine are the only thing holding me in the present. I've not been able to speak of that day for so long that I'd started to wonder whether I'd imagined it or if it had happened to someone else. No. It's all still right there, eating me from the inside.

"I swung at Arthur, ready for a fight, but I didn't realize Jaison and Greg were behind me. Greg grabbed me from behind while Arthur and Jaison unleashed punch after punch. I couldn't fight off all three of them. I tried. I tried to pull his hands from around my chest. I tried to kick. I tried everything I could."

"They were wrestling champions," she states matter-of-factly.

"Yeah," I say in acknowledgement. I hadn't known that tidbit at that moment, though I can't say I would have made different choices. I still would have tried to stop Arthur. I still would have thrown that punch. I just maybe would have gotten some help first. But that's the thing with having perfect hindsight. It doesn't mean shit for your future.

"When Greg let me go, I fell to the ground in a heap. My eyes locked on the girl's. I didn't even know her name. She hadn't been here long enough for me to learn it, but we stared into each other's eyes listening to their retreating voices. I don't know how long we lay there until footsteps returned. It might've been an hour, maybe twenty minutes. Hell, it might've been five minutes. When the footsteps stopped at my side, I knew it was the end."

I hold Vette's gaze. This next part is going to be really hard for both of us. Her lips are a tight line as she takes it all in.

"Arthur leaned real close to my ear. 'You should've minded your business. You could've waited your turn and had her too. Now, my friend, you're a liability, and we don't allow for liabilities.' He wrapped his arm around my neck and squeezed until everything went black."

Vette's hand flies to her mouth. "Oh my God, he knocked you out? What happened to the girl?"

"I don't know what happened to her. One rumor is that she was found at the bottom of the stairwell and had broken her neck in the fall. The funny thing about working on a ship is how easily replaceable we are. Her. Me. Who knows how many others simply disappeared from their positions and were replaced the next morning."

"What are you saying?"

"I'm saying that the next thing I knew, I was walking the hallway to my bunk after our mutual friends had already disembarked to find someone else using my bed, working my shift, and wearing my uniform with their own name tag on it. No one gave me a second thought, and no one has given me a second look since that night, until you. Everyone looks through me. That night cost me everything. Everything I was and everything I was meant to be."

She jumps to her knees, backing away from me, while pulling the sheet up to cover her naked body. "Are you trying to say...? No! That doesn't even make any sense."

"They killed me, Vette. They killed me and that girl that night. I don't know what happened that I'm still here and she's not. I don't know anything except this blinding hatred and anger that I've harbored all these years. I've done nothing but wander these corridors, passing between floors to look into the faces of every person who has boarded the ship, waiting and hoping for them to come back. I wanted to look them in the eye, to ask them why. When I saw them yesterday, I realized it doesn't matter. What matters is that they've been able to go on living their lives, and I've been stuck here, invisible, alone, with nothing."

I look into her eyes, silently begging her to believe me. I need her to hear my truth. There's no one else I can tell it to. There's no one else who matters. I soften my voice. "And then you saw me. I looked up in that chapel, and I could see recognition and acknowledgement in your eyes." I put my hand out, wanting to feel the crackle of air between us, wanting to know it wasn't my imagination, but she pulls back from me. She jumps to her feet and wraps the sheet around herself protectively. "I'm not going to hurt you, Odveta."

"I must still be drugged. There's no other explanation for this conversation that makes sense. You're trying to tell me you're dead, that they killed you five years ago. That...Fuck! You're saying that Arthur raped and killed another woman five years ago, and they killed you for trying to stop him. Yet, you're here! You're here in my bed. I woke up in your fucking arms. There's no way you're a ghost."

I look down, trying to think of a way to make her see the truth. "I know this is hard to believe," I say quietly before angling my face back up to hers. "I've been unseen on this ship, talking to myself, screaming at the top of my lungs, hoping someone would hear me for all these years. Yet, I still have a hard time believing it's true. The only truth I know for sure is that touching you has been the first time I've felt alive and whole since that night."

"Stop." She holds up a hand. "I don't know." She lets out a sardonic giggle. "I don't know what to believe. I remember so little about last night. I do, however, remember the chapel and how you stood behind everyone. I remember the electrical pulse between our palms when you introduced yourself on the elevator. I remember when you showed up at the cocktail hour and no one acknowledged you, even when you stood behind me with your palm on my bare skin. I simply thought...could only imagine that maybe they treated you the same way they've treated me all these years."

"Like I was invisible?" I ask.

She nods, slowly worrying her lip with her teeth. "If what you're saying is true, how is it that you block the sunlight through the window? How is it that I feel you? How is it that the only thing I can see as real is you?"

"I don't know," I say honestly. "There is something in that charge between us, like you're my polar match. Let me show you what happens when I'm not near you."

I walk to the balcony door and place my hand on the handle. Nothing happens. My hand passes straight through it. Her mouth opens in a wide circle. I smile and step through the closed glass door until I'm standing outside on the balcony, the door still sealed between us. She takes two steps forward, hand stretched, eyes wide and mouth agape. I hear a small shriek of surprise leave her throat. I step back inside and close the distance between us.

"Without you, I am literally nothing. All this time, I have subsisted on nothing more than thoughts of revenge. And here you are, my sweet vengeance, my beautiful Odveta."

She places her hands on my cheeks, and I feel that crackling, life-giving electricity flow from her to me.

VETTE

HIS SKIN IS warm against my palm, and everything in me screams to ignore what I just saw. Him walking through the unopened door reminds me of the first time we met on the elevator. I saw his hand reach between the doors as they closed, and then he was suddenly inside with me. The door never reopened, but my mind filled in the blanks, making sense of what wasn't there.

"Oh my God, they killed you!"

I don't know what to do with that knowledge. I knew they were assholes capable of so many terrible things. I knew they treated people like shit, but I never imagined them killing someone.

"And they drugged me yesterday. Holy shit!"

My knees get weak as I take in all the information he's shared with me this morning. His arms wrap around me. Prickles of static electricity travel through my body at every touch point between us.

"They have to pay for this," I say once some of my strength has returned. "We can't let them get away with it. We have to tell the cops or someone. The captain maybe?"

"Who do you think replaced me with someone else all those years ago? What do you think happened to my body or that of the young woman? There are always rumors of random deaths. Rumors that are usually wiped away with happy stories of them finding true love at a port and deciding to stay. I'm sure that many times it's an accident, but after what happened to me, I wonder."

"But they have to pay for what they did to you. What they did to her. What they tried to do to me!"

"They do, and they will. You, my sweet vengeance, are the key."

I stare at him, lost in his beautiful topaz eyes. I'm torn between doing everything I've always believed was a right and knowing that people like them don't always get held accountable for what they do that's wrong. My inner turmoil is interrupted by voices outside the door.

"Did you hear?" a woman's voice rings through.

"Hear what? What're they saying?"

"Samuel's body was found in the staff elevator."

An audible gasp comes from the second woman. "How?"

"Happened in the middle of the night. They say he was electrocuted. Burnt up like a piece of cinder."

"No way! I don't believe that."

"Believe it or not," the first woman intones, and I can hear the shrug in her voice.

I turn my eyes to Alessandro. He simply nods. A lump forms in my throat as I ask the question, "Was that you?"

"That was us," he says.

My mouth works, opening and closing, but no sound comes out. I'm not even sure the right questions to ask or whether or not I want the answers.

"Remember when I said I found you in the elevator?"

I nod in response, eyes wide. My mind tries to pierce

through the fog looking for answers, searching for memories, but it's all hazy.

"When I found you, Samuel had you in his arms, and it wasn't to hold you up." He looks directly into my eyes like he's trying to help me find the thread of truth. "Let's just say that I pulled you away from him at the same moment he put his key in the elevator lock. He never got a chance to turn that key. The charge between us was more than he could handle."

I swallow the lump, along with the bile threatening to rise in my throat. "You know this is crazy, right? Everything you're saying feels more like a fever dream than reality. I don't even believe in ghosts." My voice is now a screech. "Maybe I'm the one who's dead."

He shakes his head slowly, and his eyes grow somber as determination sets in. "As much as I love you naked, get dressed, Odveta. Let me at least prove to you that you are most definitely still alive."

ALESSANDRO

IT TAKES me longer to dress than anticipated because part of me believes Vette will hide away from me. She doesn't, and I nearly fall over putting on my pants when she drops the sheet to pull up her panties. I have to turn away before I show all my thoughts. I'm supposed to be thinking of ways to prove to her the truth of my words, and all I can think when I look at her is the truth of how much I want her.

My fingers itch to touch her, to feel those pinpricks of sensation as I run my hands over every single curve of her body until I feel her release. There's so much more to her than just beauty, but I would be lying if I say my breath doesn't catch when she twists her hair up on top of her head, exposing the skin at her nape.

"Excuse me, Mr. Ghost, you're staring."

Her voice breaks my trance, and a chuckle escapes me.

"Have you ever stared at the sunrise and pondered the creation of such beauty? When you have nothing but time on your hands, and you're on a ship in the middle of the ocean, the beauty of the sunrise deserves all your attention."

She smiles, a contemplative look on her face. "I prefer the

sunset," she says. "All the bold colors against the darkening sky, knowing they'll fade until there is little more than twinkling pulses of light. There can also be beauty in darkness."

And with that, she pulls on her tennis shoes and heads toward the door. I rush to follow her, trying to parse out meaning from her words. As we make our way down the hall, she speaks to everyone she sees—the stewards, other passengers, literally everyone. It's like she's trying to verify she can be seen. When we get on the elevator with another couple, she sparks up a random conversation about their favorite brand of flavored water. I laugh out loud as I watch her face try to remain serious in the moment. The couple eyes her with confusion but answers the question. Then she turns to me and says something as if trying to pull me into the conversation. Both of their faces draw up with suspicion, thinking she's either trying to scam them, or she's lost her mind. When she finally realizes they truly can't see me, she grabs my hand, telling me to touch her out loud. They both draw back, and when the elevator opens, they bolt. Her nose scrunches up in the most adorable way, and I burst out laughing.

"You're going to get yourself arrested on the ship," I say between breaths.

She looks at me, looks at the elevator door, and then back at me before falling into her own fits of giggles.

"It's true then. I fucked a dead man last night" Tears flow from her eyes as she continues to laugh. "You're actually a fucking ghost. I don't know what to do with that."

"Let's go somewhere less public to talk," I suggest and lead her out of the elevator toward what I know will be an empty theater.

A voice calling her name stops our progress.

"Odd...Vette," Greg says when she turns angry eyes on him. "Sorry. Old habits and all that." He puts his hands up in apology. "Glad to see you up and walking around." My hands ball into fists at the reminder of her drugged state. "You haven't happened to see Tracy this morning, have you?"

She stares at him for a moment, hands on her hips. "I haven't seen Tracy since she left me with that guy sometime last night."

"Yeah, she felt terrible about that. We hung out drinking when everyone else went off to do whatever it was they chose to do." He shrugs, as if her being left in a compromising position with a complete stranger while they all continued with their night was normal. "I walked her to her door before I went to bed, but she said she wanted to spend some time up on deck. I was exhausted and more than a little drunk, so I left her in the hall by our rooms."

"There seems to be a pattern of this group just leaving incapacitated women in random vulnerable places," Vette says, venom in her voice.

"Hey, look, I know I fucked up, but I went to check on her first thing this morning, and she's not answering her door. I thought maybe she went to check on you."

I feel rather than see Vette's anger bubbling up. Though Greg was the one who held me while the others beat me that night, I have less anger for him than the other two. She, however, is teeming with it.

"Hold it together, my beautiful vengeance," I say to her. "This is not the time or place."

She straightens her shoulders and relaxes slightly, her fists releasing. "What's the plan for today, Gregory?

His brows drift together a bit, as if he's trying to figure out her shifting emotions, but then he relaxes. "We plan to go hiking. There's a couple cliffs we saw the last time we were here that have great views."

"Is there a particular trail you took the last time?"

"Yeah. We hiked the yellow trail and will likely do the same since you women weren't with us."

"Okay," she says nonchalantly. "If I see Tracy, I'll let her know, and we'll find you all on the trail."

"Sounds good, thanks."

When he walks off, she turns back to me, fire in her eyes. "He left her to whatever fate might happen. There must've been something in the water when this group of guys was conceived. I need to find Tracy."

"Do you know where her room is?"

"Actually, yes. They all shared their connected rooms in a group text. I was the only one who got a room away from the group."

sixteen

VETTE

WHEN WE GET to their hall, it's easy to find Tracy's room. They've all decorated their doors as part of the wedding party. Of course, Constance and Jaison's door is garish. She has no concept of taste. Tracy's is the most subdued. I knock, not necessarily expecting a response. When the sound of something falling and a slight groan comes from the other side of the door, I call her name. I immediately get the feeling that something's wrong.

"Tracy, it's Vette."

The door opens slightly, but I don't see her.

"Is everything okay?"

"Come inside," she says without stepping out from behind the door.

I look back at Alessandro to make sure he's still with me, but I keep from touching him, so he can get through the door without scaring her. When I see her face, my knees buckle, and I plop down on the bed.

"Oh my God, what happened to you?"

She slowly walks to the chair against the balcony window and sits. Her mouth opens and closes and opens again.

"It's okay. Do you need to go see the doctor?"

She shakes her head. "No. It won't matter," she says quietly.

My hackles rise as I ask who did this to her. She shakes her head again, a quiver in her lips.

"I'm so glad you're okay, Vette. I was worried about you. Even after we got you out of the bar, I was worried." Her voice is soft and comes out on a sob.

Emotions war within me. "Please tell me what happened," I plead, though I'm afraid I already know the answer. She shakes her head again, and I wonder if she's simply unable to remember what happened. "Were you drugged too? Is that why you can't tell me?" Once again, that same movement of her head happens. This time, however, my emotions shift, and anger takes over. "Tracy, if you don't tell me what happened, I'm calling a steward or the doctor. Your face and shoulders are covered in bruises. You limped from the door to the chair. Who are you protecting?"

With that question, she finally looks into my eyes. Where there was once a lively woman who wanted to believe the best in others, there's now resignation and despondency.

"Myself," she says. "If he feels he can do this to me on a crowded ship in the middle of the ocean, what else might he do once we're back on land?" Her voice that was once sad and quiet is now loud and angry. "You don't need me to tell you who did this. You just want confirmation of what you already know. This or worse would have been your fate last night. It was mine because I helped you escape. I don't regret it. I don't, but I admit that had I seen this coming, I don't know if I would do it again."

With that, she breaks down in sobs. I kneel in front of her, putting my arms around her legs, not squeezing too hard because I don't know where else she's hurt. I want to be angry with her. When I came to the room, I wanted her to be okay, so I could lash out about them leaving me alone with that guy in the elevator. Seeing her now, knowing that I, at least, had someone looking out for me... My thoughts drift, and I look toward the door where Alessandro stands, his eyes reassuring. I swallow the knot that has formed in my throat. I swallow down all the soft emotions and let my anger boil to the surface.

"They will pay for this. They will pay for all of it," I state resolutely and stand.

Tracy looks up at me, her eyes full of confusion. "Only one person did this."

"He had help. For all the terrible things he's done, he's always had help or protection. They all need to pay."

"What are you going to do?"

I shake my head at her this time. "Don't worry about that. You just hang out here where it's safe. There's no need to answer your door. Let them believe what they will. They're probably too self-absorbed to notice anyway. And Monday morning, you get your ass off the ship and away from the lot of them. Don't ever look back."

She nods her head, but I see the uncertainty in her eyes. She and I both know how hard it is to get away from the circle. Hell, I'm only here on this ship because of how hard it is to stay away from this circle.

"Let's go," I say, opening the door behind Alessandro, our shoulders brushing, and my anger setting off the charge.

Tracy's gasp is the last sound I hear before the door closes shut.

I FOLLOW her in all her determined glory. She is a woman on a mission, and her anger is arousing. Our shared anger has my cock hard. As we pass a tiny alcove that holds the laundry room at the end of this deck, I grab her arm. Sparks fly, and I pull her inside, closing the door.

"What the fu…"

I don't let her finish the question before my mouth crashes on hers as I push her against the door. I take a deep breath, inhaling the air she meant to spew at me in a torrent of emotion. When her hands reach up grabbing my shirt, pulling me closer instead of pushing me away, I moan in satisfaction. Her tongue darts forward, finding mine, and I grab her hips while keeping her back against the wall. While I hold her against me, my hips roll, letting her feel how much she's excited me. She lets out a moan, letting my shirt go to fist her fingers in my hair. I trail kisses from her mouth to her chin, to her ear, and down her neck to where it meets her shoulder.

"You are so fucking beautiful, Odveta. Your righteous anger leaves me wanting to taste every inch of you." I run my tongue up her neck before I pull her earlobe between my teeth. "Fuck, you're absolute perfection."

"We have to make them pay," she pants out while her hips grind against mine.

I squeeze her breast, relishing the weight of them through her bra and shirt. Reaching behind her, I lock the door. The zing of electricity between my fingers, the metals and our touch is exhilarating. She fists both hands in my hair and pulls my mouth back to hers. I grab her ass in both hands and lift her onto the folding table.

She shrieks, "Will this thing hold us? Will it hold me?"

"It's stable enough," I say. "If you stay still."

I smirk knowing that what I plan to do to her will make it nearly impossible for her to hold still. With a smile on my face, I unbutton her jean shorts and pull them down off her hips, taking her panties with them. She doesn't argue, which either means she's gotten over the surprise of my reality, or she's so horny, she doesn't care. Either way, I dive between her legs, lapping up the sweet nectar that coats her beautiful pussy. I lick her from top to bottom and then spread her open, so her clit is on full display.

Looking up, I find her watching me, her breath held. I lay my tongue flat along her clit. She bites her bottom lip, and her nose wrinkles in the cutest way when I flick my tongue, tapping the tip of her swollen bud. A gasp leaves her mouth, and her head leans back against the wall. I love the way she responds to my touch, my synapses firing with each taste, thinking of all the ways I could possibly pleasure her. Her moans are a soundtrack to the meal I am savoring. When her breaths turn to pants, and the pitch of her moans creeps higher, I shove two fingers inside her dripping cunt. My lips latch onto her clit, pulling my name from her lips as the orgasm flows through her, and her walls clench around my fingers.

I pull my hand away, reveling at the glistening evidence of her release. She pulls it to her mouth, licking and sucking my fingers clean. I moan at the erotic look on her face. I want to drive into her right now, but I don't want us to lose more time exacting the justice we both desire. When she releases my hand, I squat to retrieve her shorts.

"I don't know if I will ever get enough of the taste of you," I say as I slide the fabric back up her legs.

"What are you doing?" she asks, desire still evident in her eyes.

"I'm getting you dressed. We have other things to do."

She looks down at my obvious arousal trying to break through my zipper, and I laugh with a shake of my head.

"It can wait. I have a feeling that watching you mete out their punishment will have me wanting you again and again and again."

I kiss her lips between each word. She smiles on the last one and pulls my bottom lip between her teeth. I reward her with a moan that is a promise.

VETTE

I CAN'T BELIEVE he stopped right there. The fact he got me off and then put my pants back on like it was nothing has me sitting here dumbfounded. I want nothing more than to feel him inside of me, and a quick glance below his waist says that he wants the same. But, his words are sobering. We're running out of time to stop these people from causing more damage. I wasn't exaggerating when I said I want all of them to pay, even if Arthur is the only one truly responsible for everything terrible that has happened—Alessandro's death, the rape and disappearance of that unknown woman, my being drugged and nearly raped, and then Tracy.

My anger simmers beneath the surface ready to lash out. We need to get to them before they leave the ship today. They'll be back aboard later, but who knows what else they can do in the meantime. Who else can they hurt? What other woman or bystander might they harm?

"Are you able to leave the ship?"

"I've not been able to on my own, no," he says somberly. "But I've also never been able to touch anyone before. I've been invisible until you came along. Maybe you're my ticket off here."

My mind starts running with possibilities. "How can we make this happen?" I ask. "You don't have a key card for them to scan, so if we're touching, and they see you, they won't be able to scan you out or back in if it works."

"What if you take my hand after you're scanned," he offers tentatively. "Unless things have changed, rarely does anyone pay attention to those who are exiting until you're halfway down the gangplank and ready to take pictures."

"Let's try it," I say. "It might be easier to get them alone off the ship anyway. Hopefully we can figure out where exactly they plan to go hiking and find them along the trail." Determination settling in again, I grab his shirt and pull him close, touching my lips to his. "We are going to stop them"

He nods in agreement and helps me down off the table. I exit the laundry first and get a sideways glance from the steward who is coming out of the room directly across the hall from the alcove. I smile and turn toward the elevator. The closer I get to the exit on deck two, though, determination fades. My palms get sweatier, and I rub them on my shorts.

"Relax, Bella. Either this will work or it won't, but you've done nothing wrong to be worried."

Because we're in a crowd, I don't say anything, just dip my head slightly for his benefit. I know he's right, but I also know that I need him. I need his support. I need to feel that jolt of energy between us to keep me going on this path I've set. I have always tried to do what was right, even when everyone around me was doing what was wrong, but I've never before tried to stop them. Part of me is afraid I won't be able to without him.

Though I've been quick to anger my entire life, I've never been a fighter. I've never actually had to fight. My size, my mouth and all its snark, and my family's position have kept me in relative safety. Relative because of the emotional damage this group of people have been able to cause for most of my life. Still, I've never fought back, never even stood my ground against them. I just always ran and hid, trying to stay as far away as possible. That all ends today.

Visions of the bruises on Tracy and knowing that could've been my fate or worse. I shake my head feeling anger tingle in my blood. They are going to know the meaning of my name. I am not an oddity or the oddball they've always thought me, that they've always called me. I am Odveta, and they will know my vengeance.

I'm pulled from my thoughts when the man in front of me asks to scan my card with little more than a passing glance. Before I can get to the open door and out into the sunlight, Alessandro squeezes my hand, and I lock my fingers with his. A child's voice behind us has me squeezing tighter when she asks her parents why the man in front of them didn't have his card scanned. Alessandro lets out a nervous chuckle, but neither of us turn around.

When we get to the place on the gangway for them to take photos, I look up at him warily. He shrugs, and we turn toward the camera. His arms wrap around my waist, and I smile. Once again, he takes my hand, and we make our way onto dry land. The smile on his face is priceless, and my heart leaps at the knowledge that this is his first time off the ship in years. That has to mean something. There has to be something in what we're doing that's right.

"Come this way," he says. "I know where they're going, and we can get their first."

I follow him without question, my hand still locked with his. In the distance, I hear someone call my name. I'm not sure who it is, and when I try to look up at the ship, I can't see anyone I recognize. I smile to myself. Let them see me whole and untouched. Let them come find me.

I'M NOT sure what I expected. Honestly, I'm not sure I'd imagined being on land again. If I had, though, I doubt I'd have pictured my body swaying as if I were still on a boat. I've heard many people say that our cruise ships are so big they don't feel the movement of the ocean, but that's not true. The size does calm the rocking some, especially on the higher decks, but when you spend most of your time in the bowels where the staff stay, you feel the swell of the ocean. You learn to move with it. Not to mention, when storms rage, we can't just go hide in our rooms and sleep until it's over. We still have to cook, clean, serve, and deal. I'd have thought that spending the entirety of five years incorporeal, I wouldn't have noticed the swaying anymore. Yet, here I am holding her hand and feeling like a drunken sailor. I need to get this feeling under control before we encounter any of the guys on the mountain trails.

Luckily, the island only has one good place for hiking. Most of the tourists stay near the beach, especially since that's where the shopping and bars are located. They come for relaxation, not for exercise. But for those who are willing to take to the trails, the other side of the island provides beautiful scenery and wild, virtually untouched spaces. One one end, there's a lagoon with a set of cliffs where the most daring can dive at their own risk. On the other, there's a steep drop off that allows you to see far in the distance to other islands. They're close enough to be seen but not to make out anything important on them or hear anything from them. Once you leave the comfort of the port, you are truly in a secluded island paradise.

We find the yellow trail easily and follow it halfway up. I pull her toward where I know the cliffside begins. I want her to see the view, and I wish I had a camera to capture her against the backdrop. She paints a stunning portrait. The wind whips her hair around her face, and she pulls it up, securing it in a messy bun at the top of her head effortlessly. I silently take her in, and she bites her lip before she turns again to look out over the sea.

Soon enough, we hear voices, and I grab her hand, pulling her to the trees' edge. Other than the trails, the forest here on the mountain is virtually untouched, which means big, log-standing trees with wide trunks. We hide behind them watching the groups of hikers make their way up to the summit where they'll likely continue down onto the other side. Very few people go to the top and just stay there or turn right around and come back. The adventurous climbers want to see everything the island has to offer. On the third group, we hear voices we recognize.

"I can't believe she ditched us," one of the women, Constance, I think, says. "She and the fucking oddball are probably hanging out somewhere being loners on the ship. Fucking ungrateful, disloyal bitch!"

"When I talked to her last night," Greg's voice rings through, "she had planned to come with us."

"Shut up, Greg," Arthur spits at him. "If you've got a hard-on for her, you should just say that. Something obviously changed her mind." Odveta tenses at my side. "As for that other bitch, none of us are surprised she decided not to come. She's always been wily, but one day she'll get caught."

"Yeah, well, Vette told me that if she found Tracy, she'd bring her, so I'm going to hang back for a bit. I'll catch up."

Arthur laughs, and the rest follow suit, their voices moving away from us. I almost feel bad for Greg as the current odd man out, but then I remember the role he's played in the group—holding me while they beat me, not doing anything to help that girl, and then leaving Tracy alone drunk. This is not guilt by association. His is a guilt of intentionally turning a blind eye and being a neglectful friend. He comes through the trees and makes his way to the cliff's edge, looking out over the sea in contemplative silence. I turn and realize Odveta is already stepping out of the treeline toward him. There's no way of stopping her without drawing attention before she's ready. There's determination in her walk, though she is relatively silent, her steps sure.

"Hello again, Gregory."

There's still about ten feet between them. A little too close for my comfort, but at least he's the one closest to the edge of the cliff and not her. He turns around completely, surprise written on his face.

"Vette, I didn't hear you coming. Is Tracy with you? Did you find her?"

Odveta stands there just looking at him before she responds with nothing more than a nod of her head. I make my way to stand next to her, not touching, not giving away my position, but close enough to protect her should something go wrong. My well-simmered anger is not for him, but he has gotten caught up in hers.

VETTE

I CAN HARDLY STAND to look at Gregory. The look of concern in his eyes pisses me off. Where was that concern yesterday? Where was the concern five years ago? How dare he look worried this morning and yet still hang out with the rest of them? I feel more than see Alessandro come to stand at my side. The electrical pulse in my body stretching to reach for him like we're magnetic ends searching for an opposite charge, but I'm glad he keeps his distance.

"Yes, I found her," I say with a snarl.

His face scrunches up and then he looks around as if trying to find her. "So where is she," he asks. "I thought you were going to bring her with you."

"She was in no condition to make the climb," I say, hands on my hips.

His head tilts to the side as he tries to process what I'm not saying. "What's wrong with her? Where did you find her?"

"You probably should've been more concerned about that when you left her alone last night.

His eyes narrow. "What are you talking about? I left her at her door."

"Yeah, well, someone else found her. Did you know he was going to want restitution for what he felt like he lost when she and Tony took me out of the bar? Did you know he was going to blame them? Did you know what he had planned to do to me had they not gotten me out of the bar? It's not like you don't know what he's capable of. It's not like you haven't been there for his other games."

His eyes go wide before they settle again. "Who was it you left the ship with earlier, Vette? I saw you walking hand-in-hand with some guy, but I wasn't sure I recognized him."

"Why does it matter?"

"It doesn't," he says with a shake of his head. "I just thought I recognized the guy from another cruise." The moment of fear has left his eyes, and he once again stands before me composed. "You still haven't told me where you found Tracy."

"She was in her room," I say calmly. He's played his hand and is afraid Alessandro might remember him.

"I knocked on her door," he says incredulously, almost defending himself.

"You probably did. But just like leaving her in the hall last night, you probably didn't wait long enough for her to get the door open. She could hardly walk and was bruised everywhere I could see. Your friend really did a number on her." His eyes widen, but he says nothing. "Just like he did to that girl five years ago." I take a step closer to him as his eyes register what I'm saying. "You know, the one who was on the floor while you held that guy they beat until he couldn't stand up anymore." I take another step toward him, and he instinctively takes a step back before looking behind him. The cliff is not the retreat he was hoping for.

He puts his hands up in a placating gesture as fear oozes from him. Still, his words are steady. "I don't know what you're talking about, Vette. I don't know what you've heard or who you've been talking to. If it was that guy you were holding hands with, he's lying. I didn't do anything. Now, I'm going to find Tracy."

He steps forward, and I step in front of him reaching out a hand for Alessandro. He grabs it, and I feel that familiar spark between us, but nothing registers on Gregory's face. I look from Gregory to the man at my side, a questioning brow raised. The look he gives me is uncertain.

"I don't know what's going on with you, but you're fucking crazy! What's with the hand and standing in my way? You're big, but you're not stronger than me. Get out of my way before I move you myself," he says. His voice has gone from calm to venomous, his eyes from fearful to angry.

The moment the threat is out of his mouth, I feel Alessandro's anger through our connected hands. There's no longer just a pulse of static electricity between us but bolts of lightning flashing. A small scream escapes Gregory's mouth as he jumps back three feet.

"You? What? How? Where the fuck did you come from?"

"I came from the ship where you left me bloody and beaten, where you left that girl raped and broken. I came from that room where you left me to die."

"Yeah we...no, they...beat you up a little bit, but you were alive when I went upstairs."

"I was, and so was she until your friend came back to finish the job."

"Vette, I didn't..."

Alessandro steps forward, cutting off his words. "Don't even say her name! You've caused enough damage. You left Tracy to be beaten and raped, and now you threaten Odveta. You may think because you didn't do that beating just held me, because you didn't do the raping just left her, that you're better than him. You're not. You're just as guilty. Even worse, you're a coward."

Gregory looks to his left and his right. He thinks to run, but before he can skirt by us, I reach out a hand. The electricity flowing between Alessandro and me latches onto him, jolting him to a halt. I step forward as his body twitches and he moves with me, taking a step back for each of mine. His eyes bulge and spittle flies from his lips. I watch him with a smile, knowing that he is just the first to feel our wrath.When I release him, his body drops to the ground along the cliff's edge. I give him a little push, and he's gone. There's no scream, no sound. It's as if he was never even here. My eyes drift out to sea, and I watch the birds with a smile on my lips.

Before I can snap back to reality, Alessandro pulls me into his arms, his hands grasping the hair at the nape of my neck, his mouth attacking mine. I let impulse take over, kissing him back with the same fervor. Pulling on the waistband of his pants, I undo the zipper.

"I need you," I say, my breathing heavy and my heartbeat erratic. "I need you inside of me now."

He groans, his erection fighting to break free as I push his pants to the ground. I squat in front of him and take his entire length into my mouth, moaning at the sensation of his tip in my throat. A string of words in Italian roll from his lips. Whether he is cursing or praising me, I don't care. I just need to feel him. I'm on fire as if the bolts of electricity we pushed into Gregory recoiled into my core. As I work his shaft, I unbutton my shorts and slide my hand into my pants, finding my clit and making quick circles. I hope my release will quench the flames burning through me. His hands grab a hold of my head as he rocks his hips back and forth, fucking my mouth with the same frenzy my fingers work on my clit, until he's repeating my name, and I'm whimpering. I can't catch my breath, and when streams of his release coat my throat, my entire body quakes with the force of my own orgasm. I can barely swallow, and my throat is raw, but I sit back on my heels with a satisfied grin. I pull my hand from my shorts, my breaths labored, as I try to get my heartbeat under control. He drops to his knees in front of me, pants still around his ankles and his limp cock out. He is also trying to catch his breath when our eyes lock. We both laugh in the most ridiculous way. It's not mirth or even happiness. It is something else that has us wrapped in each other's arms on our knees laughing like two clowns.

twenty-one

ALESSANDRO

IT TAKES us longer to get back to the ship because Vette's emotions have gone haywire. One moment, we're laughing in each other's arms, and in the next, she's sobbing. Before my mind can process that shift, her anger returns, and she's wanting to trudge up after the rest of the group. It's all I can do to keep her out of sight when other hikers climb past us and to stop her from breaking down at the reality of what happened on the cliff. I hate this war going on within her. Though Greg hadn't been my target, I feel no remorse. I'm not sure she does either. From what I can gather between her emotional shifts, her struggle is in the morally gray area between what they deserve and the reality of what we must do.

I learned a number of things up on that cliffside. One my vengeance is beautiful and strong, swift and pure. Two, I learned that there's nothing sexier than to watch her in her full determined glory when her eyes are lit with fire, electricity sparking from her fingers. Oh yes, she is glorious. Any reservations I might have had about my plan and the role she could play in it disappeared as her indignation jolted through Greg's body. She worked the electricity with abandon the same way she took my cock in her mouth afterwards, and the smile that played across her face was pure ecstasy. How anyone had gotten away with tormenting her for years is beyond me because she is the embodiment of her name, and she's a goddess.

Back in the room, I talk her into ordering some food. She hadn't eaten since early in the day yesterday. Our work is not yet done, and she will need the energy. One of the perks of being dead is that I have no need for nutrients. It's been years since I even missed the taste of food. It wasn't until I had a taste of her that I missed everything I'd had in life.

Lying next to her while she naps after her lunch, I let the moment of sad realization wash over me. This will all be over in less than 36 hours, and then she will disembark, leaving me to my eternal solitude once again. I twirl a strand of dark hair between my fingers and pull it to my nose to breathe in the delicious scent of her coconut shampoo. My senses battle for dominance, each fighting to overtake the melancholy with sensation. I drink her in from head to foot. She's taken off her shoes and her dark burgundy toes are a perfect match to her golden skin.

My eyes feast upon all her plump curves. Her solid calves lay thrown over my leg like a weighted blanket. My gaze skims up her thick thighs, and I allow my hand to follow its progress, sliding up to the cuff of her jean shorts. The stretch denim currently squeezes right under her delicious ass. I don't want to wake her, but my mouth longs to kiss right there in that crease, and my tongue begs to trail between her cheeks and tease her delicious entrances. My cock gets hard just thinking about it. Without conscious thought, I squeeze her ass, pulling her further into me until her core rubs against my hardening cock. I moan, and she clears her throat.

"Excuse me, Mr. Ghost. What are you doing?"

My embarrassment and desire are both so keen that I laugh at the absurdity of her question. "Oh my sweet vengeance, I don't think you need me to spell it out for you," I say, trying to let the flush in my ears and throat tamp down before I look up at her.

"Maybe not spell it," she says, "but you could talk me through it."

Her voice is hoarse. At first, I think it's from sleep, but when I look into her eyes, desire burns there. I smile and shift our bodies until mine is atop hers. She puts both hands on my cheeks and pulls my face close until we're breathing in each other's air.

"I should've known what you were," she says with a smile. "There was something about you those first few moments we locked eyes where you were both there and not. And then at the cocktail hour, I was so electrified by your touch that I ignored the voice wondering why I couldn't feel your breath as you whispered in my ear. Now, I feel your breath." She brings her lips within a hair's breadth of mine. "And I taste your lips." She pulls my bottom lip between hers and sucks, causing sparks to ignite between us. "And I feel a need for you I still don't comprehend." Her hips roll against my already hard cock, eliciting a groan before I capture her mouth completely and kiss her until we're both unable to breathe.

I need my vengeance in every sense of the word. I start pulling our clothes off, and she helps me make quick work of the fabric until we are skin to skin. She is everything soft where I'm hard, and the friction between us sets me on fire from the inside out. I need this woman like I've never needed anything before. I want to live for her. With that thought, I roll over, pulling her with me, reveling in the feel of her weight. The physical sensation brings a sense of calm I haven't felt in a long time. I don't know what I'll do when she leaves the ship, but I don't want to think about that. I just want to feel her now.

"Ride me. I'm yours to do with as you want."

She runs her nails down my chest and over my nipples, pulling a hiss from me. Sliding her hand between us, she grasps my cock and lifts herself until I slide into her wetness, the heat of her enveloping me as her walls squeeze me tight. The feel of her around me is divine ecstasy. When she begins to move, slowly lifting and lowering herself, her hands on my chest for leverage, I reach down and grab her ass, coaxing her to a faster pace.

"Don't go easy on me." A gasp leaves her lips. "Take what you need, Odveta. I want to feel you explode on my cock."

Her breathing is labored, and tiny moans come with each breath as I lift my hips to meet hers. She says nothing, but I feel when her arousal shifts with how wet she becomes. I hear it as our bodies come together over and over. The sound is almost as beautiful as her moans, and it coaxes me, trying to push me to my release. I lean up, using one of my hands to grab her hair and pull her mouth to mine. My tongue finds hers, and I pull her forward until she is laying all of her delicious weight on my chest, her ass in the air. I bend my knees and piston my hips, plowing into her, our steady rhythm growing in intensity.

"That's it, Bella," I say against her ear, not slowing my pace. My own breaths are erratic, as I force myself to hold back and wait for her. "You feel so good around my cock, squeezing me as you get closer. Are you gonna come for me?"

I slap her ass as if to punctuate the question, and she barely gets out half of my name before she clenches me tightly. Her pulsating waves take over, and her moans of release are a symphony to my ears. The crack of electricity as she milks my own orgasm from me sets off the fire alarms. We don't move as our breaths regulate and our heartbeats level out. Finally, the alarms stop.

"You are an angel," I say between breaths.

She rolls off of me, and I go with her halfway, my half-limp cock between us. I lay my hand on her lower belly, massaging the soft skin, relishing in the fact that I can touch and grab her everywhere. I slide my hand between her legs, and she sucks in a breath when my fingers find her swollen nub, still sensitive from her orgasm. Still, I push lower to where she is soaked from both of our releases. Her mouth opens, and a soft gasp leaves her as I plunge two fingers inside. I growl with satisfaction, my lips clamping onto her nipple.

"I bet you taste absolutely delicious right now."

As soon as the words have left my lips, I slide my fingers out of her and place them on my tongue with a moan of pleasure.

"Were you always such a gentleman," she asks. My head cocks to the side, not quite sure I understand her question. She giggles. "Most men leave us to clean up ourselves, but you sound like you want to clean me with your tongue."

A small chuckle leaves my lips. "Are you a mind reader now?"

"Only when our minds are of one accord." I smile at her choice of words. "I would, of course, reciprocate."

My smile grows, and I lick my lips at the thought. "We still have a lot to do today," I say.

"This is true. But since the ship hasn't left port yet, we have time."

I laugh a full-belly laugh and lay back on the bed. "Then put that pretty pussy on my face."

She takes no time turning herself around to put her knees on either side of my chest. She hovers her ass above my face, and I lean up to lightly nip at the skin of her inner thigh. She rewards me with a little moan. My vengeance doesn't mind a little pain with her pleasure. I repeat the action on the other side, and this time her groan is a complaint.

"If you want my mouth, sit that pussy all the way on my face. No hovering." I say those last words with a commanding tone to let her know I'm serious. She won't get what she wants unless I also get what I want.

"I don't want to smother you," she responds, and her concern is cute.

"My sweet vengeance, you forget I'm already dead. Let me live a little."

With that, I wrap my hands around her body, grab her ass cheeks and spread them apart. Pulling her down onto my face, I bask in the sweetness. When her lips wrap around my cock, nothing else matters.

IT'S hours before we leave the bed again. The others should be back by now, but we decide to wait until the ship moves out to sea before seeking them out. Instead, we sit on the balcony. Voices float up to us as passengers make their way back onto the ship. Finally, we hear ones we recognize.

"I can't find him anywhere," Jaison's voice drifts up from the dock. "He wasn't on the trail or on any of the cliffs."

"I couldn't find him either." That's Francesca.

The ship's horn blasts a warning that we'll be leaving soon.

"He's probably on the ship asleep in his room. Or maybe he finally found Tracy and got his cock wet. Either way, he knows the rules, and we can't change them. We have to be back on the ship by the time they close the door. I'm not willing to miss the boat for him."

"Leave it to Constance to think of herself first," I say quietly, so my voice doesn't carry down to them.

"Babe, he's our friend," Jaison argues.

"Are you willing to get stuck here and leave me on the ship by myself on our wedding weekend?" she asks, sarcasm evident in her question. She knows he's not. The lot of them are too selfish for any of that.

"I'm willing to bet he's on the boat," Arthur says. "He probably blew off some steam from our earlier conversation and then decided not to join us at all. He can be a real punk sometimes."

I can almost see the eye roll, so I don't look over the balcony to see them.

"You're probably right," Jaison says, finally acquiescing. "Let's go ahead and get on the ship."

Their voices grow faint, and I turn to look at Alessandro. I hadn't thought about it earlier, but there was one voice I didn't hear on the island.

"Did you notice that no one mentioned Tony? I didn't hear him on the island either."

Alessandro looks at me with a raised eyebrow. "I hadn't, but it is interesting, isn't it? In fact, the last I saw of him, he and Constance had gotten into an argument. She wanted to fuck him like the icing on her wedding cake. Sweet but no substance to the relationships, and he wasn't happy about it."

"Oh my God, the poor guy still thinks he could one day be the one she chooses." I shake my head. He's been pining after that bitch since middle school.

"Well," Alessandro says, leaning over and kissing my neck right below my earlobe, "based on the conversation I heard, he's as enthralled with her as I am with you. They've been having an affair just like Francesca and Jaison."

"Yeah, I'm surprised Arthur let that go on," I say.

"I don't think he knows."

I process that thought for a minute. "That's something we might be able to use against them, but it doesn't answer the question about Tony."

"No, it doesn't."

twenty-three

ALESSANDRO

WE AGREE that since I can pass through the ship invisibly, I'll go off to find everyone's location. It isn't hard to find the two couples together at dinner. Their laughter and arguments continue to be obnoxiously loud.

"Why are we still talking about them?" Constance asks.

Her voice is shrill, nothing like the melodious voice of my Odveta. I need to stop thinking of her as mine when she'll be gone after tomorrow, but it's hard. She is everything I could've ever wanted, like she was perfectly made for me. If only I were able to be the man she deserves. Francesca's voice breaks me from my thoughts when she mentions Odveta.

"Why are you so worried about Vette anyway?" She directs the question at Arthur. "You're almost as obsessed with her as Greg was with Tracy this morning. What the fuck do you care? It's not like you're fucking her or something." She scoffs. "Imagine that."

Arthur scowls at her. "No, I'm not fucking her."

But you want to, I think to myself as my fists clench. It's a good thing Odveta is not here. All my anger would be showing our hand. That was the other thing I learned on the island. The sparks between us are simply our connection, but our combined anger gives me physical shape for everyone to see. It's too late for them at that point.

"Last night was enough. We showed her who's boss and still in charge. Leave it alone and let her go hide off in her hole again," Francesca continues. He sneers at her.

"Speaking of Greg, he still hasn't shown up." "Nor has Tracy," Jaison and Constance chime in.

"Who gives a fuck," Arthur says. "At the end of the day, we are the only four that matter. They'll come running back to us soon enough."

"You're such an asshole sometimes, dude," Jaison says, but then he lifts his cup in a toast and finishes his drink.

Still, there's no mention of Tony from any of them. I walk away through the server who happens to be standing behind me, and he shivers, nearly dropping the tray of food in his hands. I make my way down to the deck with their rooms. Even though I've been invisible all this time, I'm still not comfortable with passing in and out of passengers' rooms. Somewhere in my mind, I still believe in giving them privacy whether they know I'm there or not. But, I need to find Tony's location to ensure he doesn't interrupt what we have planned. I need to find him to ensure he receives his punishment for the danger he put Odveta in.

I start with Tracy's room since I know that one. Sneaking my head in, I see she's asleep. Her breathing is calm, and I'm relieved. Though she had a hand in Odveta being in danger last night, she had tried to help and suffered for it. She doesn't deserve any more suffering. I move to the next decorated room, the one with the big bride and groom on the door, tulle standing out halfway into the hall. This is obviously Jaison and his new wife's room, but I promised to check everywhere for Tony. There's no one inside, and the room is a mess. I feel sorry for their steward.

It looks like everyone on this trip decided to get a balcony room, as they're all on the same side of the hall. The next room has signs that say Maid of Honor and Best Man. I doubt I'll find Tony here either, but I still make my way inside. This room is much neater, though there's a pile of wet clothes on the bathroom floor. I recognize the color of the shirt as the one he was wearing last night. He must've tried to wash the blood out. That's the only explanation I can figure for why his clothes are wet on the floor. I notice, though, that there's a second shirt and what looks like two pairs of shorts. It doesn't make sense that he would've felt the need to wash out two sets of clothes for one night with Tracy.

I leave the room and head to the next one. This one is Greg's. I recognized his clothes from yesterday at the bar. I thought I might feel some emotion going into the man's room, but there's nothing. He was nothing. I make it to the final room of the group and listen carefully at the door. I don't hear anything and peek my head in. I don't see much, but the room has obviously been tidied. That means, he hasn't been here since the steward cleaned it. He isn't with the group. He's not with Tracy. Where in the hell can he be?

Taking one more look around, I notice something outside on the balcony. There's a smudge on the banister. What the hell? Stepping through the glass door, I take a closer look. The banister was obviously wiped down but not very well as there's a rust-colored smear on it. I look around, my mind trying to put pieces of the puzzle together. Blood on the banister and a missing man can only mean one thing, but the questions of how and why play over in my mind. Two sets of wet clothing.

Arthur beating the shit out of and raping tracy for protecting Odveta. Arthur leaving that woman bloody and broken before coming back to finish the job. Everything comes back to Arthur, and my blood boils. I need to get back to my avenging angel. No one else can suffer at the hands of that man.

twenty-four

VETTE

ALESSANDRO COMES THROUGH THE DOOR, and I give a shriek of surprise. Though I know and have accepted that he's a ghost, I don't know that I will ever get used to him showing up out of nowhere. I start to laugh, to tell him that he scared the shit out of me, but then I see the anger in his face, and mine falls.

"What's wrong? What did you find?"

He comes into the room and pulls me into his arms. Some of his tension releases as warmth spreads between us with the electrical charge.

"Tracy wasn't the only one punished for helping you last night."

I pull back from him to look into his eyes. I shake my head. "Who else? Did you find another woman somewhere? Is he a serial rapist?"

Alessandro puts his hands on my shoulders. "I don't know how prolific his violence against women is, but I do believe that Tracy and Tony are the only reason you are still alive right now. I'm also fairly certain Tony is not."

I gasp, a hand going to my chest. I was angry at him for

having left me alone with that man. Still, I sympathized with him still yearning for Constance and her treating him like a toy. I feel like of all the men, he was the only one with a conscience. To think he possibly died because of that conscience makes my heart ache. To think it happened because he helped me makes me angry. I did not deserve whatever Arthur had planned. Tracy did not deserve what Arthur did to her. If he indeed hurt Tony, that was also undeserved. The only one who deserves to be hurt for what they've done is him.

"Arthur has to pay," I say without hesitation."He must be stopped. There shall be no redemption for him."

"Yes," Alessandro says, his voice steadfast. "We will end this tonight."

WE EASILY FIND them back in the sports bar. It is hard for either of us to contain our anger right now, so I keep my distance from her, enough to keep myself invisible. She finds a place in the doorway that is directly in Arthur's view. Our plan is to get him away from the others. They deserve their own punishment, but he deserves so much more. I see in his face the moment he notices her. His eyes open wider and a smile forms on his lips. When she turns and walks away, a sneer forms from that smile before he gets out of the booth and follows her.

"Where are you going?" Francesca says at his back, but he doesn't answer. What the fuck is wrong with him lately," she asks loudly, drawing attention from others in the bar.

"Let him go. You're embarrassing us," Constance says before pulling Jaison's mouth to hers for a kiss. Jaison's eyes are locked on Francesca.

I follow Arthur, leaving the rest of them to their game. I cannot trust Arthur alone with Odveta. He's like a predator, and I will make sure he soon realizes he is the prey tonight. Odveta leads him through a series of turns. She makes her way outside and down the stairs to the next deck where he can easily see her. She walks fast enough to give him the sense that she is trying to get away and yet doesn't leave his sight. I walk alongside him watching his face, inwardly shaking my head at how predictably he's behaving. His confidence in being able to do whatever he wants is at an all-time high, and that arrogance will play to our advantage.

She makes her way down the halls, ducking into different stairwells, constantly heading downstairs. I quickly catch up with her, steering her to the destination we chose. I wonder if he will remember the spot, but when he turns the corner, there's no acknowledgement on his face. The only thing there is malice and pride, as if he won the cat and mouse game by cornering her.

"You won't get away from me this time, Oddity. I'm tired of playing this game with you. It's time I earned the spoils of the hunt."

Pride swells in me when she raises a brow. She doesn't cower, doesn't even look my way. She is vengeance, and I am nothing more than her tool.

"Look around, Arthur," she says. "I have spent over a decade avoiding you, avoiding being alone with you. Do you think I would let you corner me at the bottom of the ship?"

"I think you made a wrong turn. I think you're not as smart as you think you are. I think had you not had help getting away from me last night, it wouldn't have mattered where you ended up tonight. The game would have ended then. Your luck has run out."

She puts a finger to her mouth in mock contemplation, and I almost feel sorry for him. "Do you know where you are?" she asks.

"What does it matter?" He takes a step forward, but she doesn't step back any further into the open room.

"Do you recognize this place?"

He looks around quickly, and shakes his head with a shrug. "No."

"So you're never haunted by the vision of two broken bodies on the floor covered in blood?"

His brow raises and a questioning look comes over his face as he looks around again. Then his eyes open wide. "What do you think you know?" he asks.

Her face is a mask of indifference. "I know that you're an absolute asshole. I know that you're a danger to others. I know that you'll do whatever you feel is needed to get what you want. And I know I'm done running."

"Good because I'm tired of the chase."

He starts to unbuckle his belt. This arrogant asshole actually believes she means to submit to him. He doesn't think the location is significant enough. He doesn't care or even acknowledge his actions of the past couple days. Yet, he thinks she'll submit. My blood boils when he pulls his belt out and wraps it around his hand. I don't even let him step forward before I grab Odveta and pull her into my arms.

"You will not touch her," I say, watching Arthur's eyes go wide with shock as he stumbles backward.

"What the fuck? Where the fuck did you come from?" he says aloud. "Get the fuck out of here and mind your damn business." His voice booms within the metal-walled room.

"Oh no, not this time Arthur. This time, you are alone. You will not rape another woman." Arthur's brow creases at my words. "You will not kill another man for standing up against you," I say.

His brows draw down and his head tilts to the side as he looks me up and down. "Who are you?"

"What happened to Tony?" Odveta asks.

Arthur turns his gaze on her, his face darkening. "Why are

you asking me about Tony? He couldn't mind his fucking business any more than this dude."

"What did you do to him? Did you beat him within an inch of his life and then finally kill him, like you did in this room five years ago? You seem to have a pattern, Arthur," Odveta says. Her anger has risen to match mine, and the hair at my nape stands with the charge flowing through us.

"How do you know what happened five years ago?" Fear creases his brow.

"Because a ghost told me," she says without a hint of laughter, and then she releases my hand.

Arthur blinks multiple times, taking a step back again trying to get his bearings. "What the fuck? Where'd that guy go? What's happening here?" He looks around, but never turns his back on her. "You stupid bitch, you don't know anything. Nothing happened here five years ago, but even if it had, it won't matter. You won't be telling anyone anything after tonight."

"That's the first accurate thing you've said all night. I won't be telling anyone else because you'll no longer be a danger to anyone. You won't matter anymore." Her anger is lightning, bouncing off every surface of the room, tickling the air around Arthur until his hair stands on end.

ARTHUR STANDS TRANSFIXED, and I see uncertainty in his eyes for the first time since we met as kids. I relish his fear. After all these years of running and hiding from him without any idea the length he'd go to, I finally know how the game will end.

"How many women have you harmed, Arthur? Francesca not enough for you that you have to force other women to fuck you?"

His eyes harden, and his nostrils flare, but he doesn't move.

"How does it feel to know that I've let a ghost fuck me? How does it feel to know that he's touched everything you've been obsessed with for years? How does it fucking feel to know that you are so insignificant that I would rather give myself to a memory than you?"

His breathing is heavy, and his anger is palpable, but the fear is still there...and it's delicious.

"I'll kill you. I'll kill you and then fuck every hole in your fucking corpse, you fucking bitch."

He says the words, and I believe he means them, but the fact he still hasn't taken a step forward has a smile spreading across my face. I take a step toward him, and his eyes widen. Another step, and he retreats. I raise a brow.

"What happened, Arthur? I thought you wanted nothing more than to fuck me...to rape me...to kill me. All these years of running from you and your obsession, and you're nothing more than a coward who preys on those weaker than you or gets his friends to level the playing field." I shake my head, disgusted. "This all ends tonight," I say, reaching out a hand toward Alessandro.

My anger crackles through the room on its own, but he deserves to have a hand in this as well. I may be his angel of vengeance, but he is the one whose life was forfeit to this man. Sparks fly everywhere when we touch, our shared anger and hatred combining. Arthur, for his part, doesn't try to run. He stands there looking between us watching the sparks bounce off the walls, imagining the gauntlet he'll have to pass through to run.

"Do you no longer feel the strongest man in the room?" I ask, a sardonic smile on my face.

Turning to face Alessandro, her finally says, "I killed you before, you fucking corpse. I can do it again," but insecurity has crept into his voice. There's a slight tremble in his lip.

"You brought us together," Alessandro says, taking a step closer to him. "I've waited five years to look you in the eye. For all these years, I've thought about all the things I'd say to you, all the things I wanted to do to you for what you had done. None of those compared to the thoughts I had when we saw Tracy and knew what you had planned to do to Odveta." He takes another step forward, and I see the moment Arthur decides to swing at him.

I try to scream the words 'watch out,' but no sound leaves my mouth. All I hear is static, our electricity coursing through me, and I push the current of energy through Alessandro. His hand goes up, connecting with Arthur's fist, and a scream gets caught in Arthur's throat as his body gives over to the charge.

"First, you will burn here," Alessandro says, "and then you will burn in hell."

Smoke comes from Arthur's mouth. I watch, unmoving and unfeeling, unlike when my hands provided the shock to Gregory. I don't feel the exhilaration. I feel nothing. Even as his clothes catch fire, there is no remorse. I pull on Alessandro's hand, until he looks at me. The fire burning in his eyes concentrates every pinprick of sensation between my legs. He lets go of Arthur, whose lifeless body immediately crumbles to the floor. I give him no more thought as Alessandro's hands are all over me.

He pushes me against the wall. In a heartbeat, my shorts are gone, his pants are around his ankles, and my legs wrap around his waist. I barely register that he is able to hold me up as he pounds in and out of me, working through the energy coursing between us until we're both on fire. I cry out into his mouth where our tongues are entwined, and he follows me seconds later. Once our clothes are back in place, we step over Arthur's body. Without a second look, we make our way back to my room to clean up.

twenty-seven

ALESSANDRO

I SIT on the balcony waiting for Odveta to get out of the shower. My mood is, well, I'm not really sure. I thought that finishing things with Arthur would have brought me peace, but that's not where I am. It's a weird state of melancholy, as if I no longer have a purpose. My soul has been wandering with nothing else but a plan for retribution, and now that it's over, what do I do next? And what do I do with these feelings for Odveta knowing she'll be leaving the ship tomorrow?

I can't ask her to stay. There's nowhere for me to hide her on the ship. Though I was able to leave the ship with her to go onto the island, I can't imagine asking her to spend the rest of her life with me as a ghost. That wouldn't be fair. She would want to be able to experience life with her partner, not hide away because his life is already over. I couldn't ask her to do that. So here I sit, wondering what's to happen next.

I know she's watching me before she even opens the balcony door. My spirit responds to her nearness much the same way my body responds to her touch, with tiny pinpricks. Just enough to remind me how it feels to be alive. I think that's the hardest part. It's like when you sit in one position too long, and your foot or hand falls asleep. It's the tiny prickles of pain as the numbness wears off that tell you that body part is still not quite functioning. That's how I feel, like I've been numb for years and am now being tortured with tiny pinpricks promising an awakening that will never happen.

"Hey," she says, wrapping her arms around my neck from the back.

"Hello yourself."

"Are you alright?"

"I was going to ask you the same thing."

"Truthfully, I'm not sure," she says quietly. "I thought I would feel bad, you know? But, I don't. Arthur deserved to die. Gregory was a danger to others. That man in the elevator, the one who planned to rape me likely would've done so to other women if he hadn't already. Bullies and predators don't stop. But I thought, at least I always imagined, there would be guilt if I were to ever take someone else's life."

"I know."

I don't say anything else. There's nothing I can add that will change that feeling for her. Most people think it morally wrong to take another life. They fear the guilt and repercussions preemptively. But most people aren't in a position to enact vengeance on others. They've not lived through their own murder. Odveta's anger wasn't so much for herself. She's an avenging angel looking out for others. Knowing she also suffered, the work feels incomplete to me.

"What about the rest of the group?" I ask. "Do we let them off the hook? All the years they tormented you. Jason's hand in protecting Arthur and supporting his terrible acts. The women who put you in this position this weekend and drugged you into submission. Do we just let that go now?"

She stands and walks around the chair on the small balcony before taking a seat on my lap. I pull her close, turning her sideways, so her feet lay over the arm of the chair and dangle into the other seat.

"Will it change anything?" she asks quietly. "Will it let us stay like this together?"

That question has my throat tightening, and a tear streams down my cheek. I wipe it away before she can see it and manage to croak out a noncommital response.

"What's going to happen when I have to leave this ship?" Her voice is sad.

"You pack your things and get scanned out the same as you had planned to do when you got here."

"I don't mean for me." She turns to look up at me, and I close my eyes before she can see the tears rimming them. "Alessandro, look at me. What will happen to you? What about us?" She pauses before saying the last word.

There's something strange about saying 'us' when one of us barely exists. "I'm not really here, Bella. I'm a ghost, a specter, only made whole by your touch." I can't keep the sadness out of my voice, but I also can't lie. "You're still alive and not meant to hide in the shadows."

"I've spent my whole life hiding," she says. "These people, this group, had me hiding forever. But you see me, all of me. I don't want my life to go back to what it was. I don't want to give them that power back. And, I don't want to lose the feeling that runs along my skin and explodes in my veins when we touch. This energy, this electricity between us...I need it."

"You deserve to be able to step out into the world and not have to answer a million questions. I can't give that to you. Greg, Jaison, and Arthur took that possibility away from me. But, I also don't want to be here without you," I say, pulling her close and kissing her hair. "I don't want to go back to being invisible and alone, a wandering soul. I thought I had spent all these years wandering in search of the opportunity for my revenge when what I was really searching for was an opportunity to live again. You've given me both, and the thought of losing it all is its own brand of hell."

"Then don't," she says, turning back to look at me. She rearranges herself, so she is straddling my legs. "Don't let me go. Hold onto me. Be whole with me. Don't let me go back to hiding. We can finish this. There's still one more responsible for your death and two more for my years of torment, not to mention everything that happened this weekend. We'll finish what we started and then figure out how to start something new. This spark between us isn't meant to just fizzle out." Emotion colors the last sentence before determination sets her jaw again.

I agree, knowing I would do anything for her. Together, we will fan the flames of this spark into a new life. "Let me go find them," I say as we stand to go back in the room.

HE COMES BACK MAYBE thirty minutes later with a smirk on his face. "They're at the back of the ship in a hot tub together. I have never seen a group of friends so quickly and easily forget about each other," he says incredulously. "Four of them have gone missing, but they sit up in a hot tub."

"Jason and Constance are perfect for each other," I state matter-of-factly. There is no surprise for me. "And Francesca is the perfect lap dog for them both."

I can hear them before we even turn the corner. Both women are giggling, and then I hear Jaison's voice. "You know, ladies, we could have some fun here in this hot tub." There's a splash of water and then a slap.

"We just got married, Jaison. You're already trying to fuck my best friend on our honeymoon?"

I look at Alessandro with an eyebrow raised, and he just shakes his head. There is no saving them.

"I was just saying that if you two had ever considered, you know...now would be a good time."

"We've done it before," Francesca says. "Back in college."

"What?" The surprise in Jaison's voice nearly makes me

laugh aloud, and I have to throw my hands over my mouth to keep from letting them know we're here.

"You said you'd never tell anyone," Constance complains.

"Yeah, but he's your husband, and he was asking for something you won't give him. I just thought he deserved to know why."

I peek around the corner and see Jaison's head give that questioning tilt. "We've known each other for how long and been fucking since high school. How did I not know you two had hooked up?"

"No one was supposed to know. We were out of the country, at a party, and drunk. There was this really hot guy, and he asked to have both of us. I thought he was just gonna fuck us one at a time."

"Her selfish ass," Francesca pipes in, "thought she wouldn't have to do anything besides just take it. He, however, was deliciously dominant and expected so much more."

Well now, I think to myself. This is getting interesting. Alessandro looks just as fascinated as I am.

"You've got to be kidding me. All these years I've imagined you two sucking my cock together, and you're telling me that you gave that to some random dude in a bar?"

"Oh, we gave him more than that," Francesca admits, a proud smirk on her face.

"Shut the fuck up! He doesn't need to know. It was just that one time." Constance is whining now.

"It may have only happened that one time, but you've looked at me differently ever since. I see how you watch my ass and how you find a reason to come into my dressing room when we're out shopping. Just like with everything else, you're too much of a cowardly bitch to ask for what you want."

Oh shit. My eyes widen in surprise. Maybe Francesca's not the lapdog. I look over at Alessandro, and intrigue is written all over his face. Both of us stand there silently, waiting to see what happens next.

"I won't give you all the delicious details, Francesca says, but I'll tell you her favorite part."

"Cesca, no," Constance pleads as though she knows it's too late to stop Francesca telling all her secrets.

"I've always done everything you wanted, C. I've been your best friend. I've been your stepping stone. I've been your lapdog and your scapegoat. I've done all the little things you've been too afraid to do, like slipping that drug into Vette's drink the other night. And what have I gotten in return?" Francesca is standing in the middle of the hot tub at this point in her rant. "A boyfriend who would rather chase after everyone else, so he can get off on the power of fucking women who don't want him? Or maybe memories of the best fucking night of my life with you that I can't even talk about because you're too much of a coward to admit that you're strongest orgasm came while you were eating my pussy? Anyway, I just wanted to let your husband know that if we are the wedding gift he wants, I'm not the reason he can't have it."

I step out from around the corner clapping my hands. "This is the most brilliant soap opera I've ever watched," I say, laughter in my voice. "Does Arthur know? After all the horrible things he's done for no good reason, I can't believe he would have let you all live had he known that you not only fucked your best friend with someone else but that you've also been fucking his best friend all this time." A screech flies out of Constance as she lunges for Francesca.

"You stupid bitch," Jaison spits at me. "What the fuck did you do that for? Why are you even here?"

"Because none of you deserve to be happy."

I can tell by the look on his face that he's taken aback by my statement. Confusion is etched in his brows, and the two women stop their tussling.

"Regardless of the shit going on between the three of you and the torment you put me through for years, the worst part is how shitty you all are to each other. The fact that you don't seem to care that four people in your group are missing is unbelievable to me." I walk back and forth in front of the hot tub laying out all their indiscretions. "Constance, did you know that your husband and his friends were on this ship five years ago and beat the shit out of a man who tried to stop Arthur from raping and killing a woman?"

Francesca's mouth falls open. "Oh, you didn't know that about your guy either, you self-absorbed piece of shit?" I ask her. "I guess you also didn't know that his plan for this weekend was to rape me. That thought never crossed your mind when you drugged me? Hmmm, maybe you just didn't care. Like you couldn't seem to care less that he raped and beat the shit out of Tracy for helping me escape the bar that night."

They all gasp. "Yeah, she's in her room, hardly able to walk. But, at least she's in her room, unlike poor Tony. Arthur threw him off the ship because he helped me."

"You're lying," Constance says. "There's no way. I just saw him last night."

"Yeah, well, Arthur had a lot of free time on his hands when he couldn't find me, and your husband was too busy fucking Francesca to keep him calm." She looks back and forth between Jaison and her best friend, a combination of hurt, anger, and disbelief on her face. "Maybe you shouldn't have let Tony walk away when he no longer wanted to be your fuck toy."

"What in the every loving fuck is happening here?" Jaison asks. "Where is Arthur? We're gonna get to the bottom of this."

"You don't have to worry about him. He won't hurt anyone ever again."

"What do you mean?" His face pales.

"I'm pretty sure I said it clearly. He will never hurt anyone again, and neither will you," I say, reaching out to grab Alessandro's hand while simultaneously plunging mine into the hot tub.

The already bubbling water begins to boil, and they start flailing. My eyes widen at the sudden finality of it all. With them, there was no moment of extreme anger. It remained a constant simmer right under the surface, a simmer born of years of bullying that led to fear, hiding, and insecurity. Rather than wrath, this is anger wrapped in sadness, knowing that this is the end. This group is the reason Alessandro and I never got a chance to find each other in life.

At this moment, I want to burn the whole ship down. I want to watch the flames engulf it. I pull my hand from the water and wrap my arms around him, tilting my head up for a kiss. Unlike our previous moments of abandon, this kiss is soft and slow, full of emotion. At least we have tonight to spend wrapped in each other, and in the morning, we'll decide what comes next. I break the kiss and grab his hand.

"Let's go back to the room," I say, walking us off the deck that now smells like burning wire.

twenty-nine

ALESSANDRO

THERE'S a pit in my stomach, an ache that I can't quite name. The relief at knowing our work is done is tainted by the movement of the ship toward its home port. We walk silently through the corridors and down the stairs, not rushing to take the elevator. She never releases my hand, and I unconsciously rub my thumb over hers. The tiny bit of friction reminds me that she's still here, and for the moment, she's mine.

Passengers have begun setting their suitcases out into the hall for pick up, so we maneuver ourselves around them. The hour is late, and we see very few passengers. Instinctively, I make eye contact with a few men we pass before I remember they think she's alone. One man nods in my direction, at least I imagine he's nodding at me. Maybe Odveta acknowledged him, and I didn't notice.

On her hall, a couple walks in our direction. I think to release her hand and move out of the way. Although they can walk right through me, it's uncomfortable for both of us when it happens. Their shiver and my emptiness make me feel even more hollow. Odveta, however, doesn't release my hand, just holds me close to her. I take a deep breath, ready for the sensation when the couple separates. The woman walks in front of the man as they both squeeze to the side to get around us. "Excuse us," the woman says, and he acknowledges me with a nod. I turn my head to watch them, but they don't give me a backwards glance. I look at Odveta. She doesn't register anything, just keeps her eyes on the ground. Just what I need, to lose my mind after all this.

She opens the door to the room and pulls me inside. When the door closes, I pull her toward me, turning her to face me and use my finger to lift her chin. Tears fill her eyes, and her lashes are clumped together with the dampness of them. I kiss each eye, tasting the saltiness of her tears before kissing her lips. Slowly, we undress each other, our hands and mouths weaving a tapestry of emotion. Our electricity still sizzles beneath the surface, but there's no explosion of sparks, just the friction of our bodies touching. We spend most of the day wrapped in each other, pretending time isn't against us.

In the quiet stillness, she lay staring into the darkness with her head on my chest. "I don't wanna let you go," I finally muster the courage to say.

"I'm not leaving you," she says, her voice more controlled than mine.

"You can't stay on the ship, Odveta. They won't let you."

"The biggest lesson I learned this weekend," she says, "is that I refuse to let others determine my life or my happiness. I don't want a life without you."

I bite my lip to hold back the sob threatening to come at her words. "I can't ask you to give up your life. Not for me. Not for anything. Just knowing you exist makes the world a better place and a whole lot less lonely."

"You can come with me," she offers, hope evident in her voice.

"What kind of life would you have with an invisible man, a broken soul?"

"I would have you. I would have this." She leans up, her hands against my chest. "this feeling between us. This spark. I can't imagine not feeling you. Please," she implores, and I sit up to face her. I take her face in my hands and kiss her lips. I feel wetness when our faces touch, but I don't know if the tears are hers or mine. "I need you," she says.

I stare at her. She's barely visible in the dark, yet I see every inch of her. The sliver of determination in her eyes is on full display. She means every word. "I need you too," I respond, pulling her back down to lie in my arms. My mind plays through a million scenarios, and in every one of them, she eventually regrets this decision, resents this moment, and my heart is broken. Still, I can't tell her no. "I'll come with you," I say. "Now get some sleep."

thirty

ALESSANDRO

THE FIRST GLINT of sunlight comes through the window, and I run my fingers through her hair. She still sleeps soundly, and I'm not ready to wake her, not ready for reality to set in. Though we agreed to leave the ship together, I know things will not end the way we expect them to.

I throw the covers off and slide my arm out from underneath her head to rise. The ship has stopped moving, which means we're already in port. I usually stay below deck on port days not wanting the reminder that I was stuck here. Today, armed with the knowledge I'll be walking off of this ship forever, I open the balcony door and step outside. The ship's crew is busy locking things down, connecting the gang plank, and preparing to take on new supplies for the next voyage.

I used to love the hustle and bustle of these days and the challenge of getting everything done in time for the new passengers to board. Soon the streams of people, some with luggage, and some without, would be filtering out into the port. Then things would start all over again with the new throng making their way onto the ship as we finished preparations. For the first time in years, I'm nostalgic for that busyness, for those passing conversation with the others as we'd run back and forth to get things done. I felt most alive on those days because of the challenge and the way I would fall into my bunk exhausted at the end of the day.

I'd not felt alive in so long, not until Odveta. She brings new life to my soul and has allowed me this moment to remember what I once enjoyed about being on the ship. A single tear rolls down my cheek, and I wipe it away. There's no sense in crying over what was anymore.

"There's a lot of people down there, aren't there, Mister?" a small voice says.

I look around to see two small eyes peeking through the slats of the balcony. They're staring at me, and I respond affirmatively without thinking. "Today is a busy day on the ship."

"Do you all go home now? My mom says that we'll be going home today."

I look at the small boy. Though I can't see him fully, I imagine he's five or six years old. "Do your parents know you're out here?"

"No, they're still sleeping. They didn't come back to the room until real late. I pretended to be asleep, and they were talking about how people got hurt in an electrical fire."

"Oh really?" I say, trying to mask how much I want him to tell me more.

"Yeah, they were talking about how scary it is to have a fire on the ship and that maybe we won't ever come back on a big boat again."

"It can be scary to have a fire on the ship."

"Yeah, because what if everything burns down, and we end up in the water? What if we can't swim?"

"Well, if you look through the glass in front of you and down a little bit, you'll see some big yellow pods."

"Where?"

"Right underneath us. They stick out the side."

"Oh yeah, I see them. They have yellow and white and red."

"Those are little boats and get all the people off the ship safely."

"Really?"

I laugh a little at his excitement. "Yes."

"So we don't have to be afraid to come back on the big boat. I really like it here. It was a lot of fun and there was good food all the time."

I smile before the balcony door opens slightly. "Who are you talking to?" Odveta asks. I look up to see her eyes shining. Her dark hair cascades around her shoulders, covering her beautiful breasts. If my new friend with the wide eyes wasn't out here, I'd pull her outside and make good use of this balcony.

"My little friend here. We were watching the crew do their work of turning over the ship for the next group of passengers."

"Good morning," she says, peeking her head out of the door without showing the rest of her.

"Good morning. My name is Jonah."

"It's very nice to meet you, Jonah. My name is Vette."

"It's really Odveta," I say, "which is too beautiful to be shortened. Don't you agree?"

"It's a different name."

"It is as unique as she is."

"Mommy says I was named after this guy who got swallowed by a whale. I tried to tell her whales don't eat people, but she says that's what happened in the story. I don't believe it."

Odveta and I both chuckle at him. "I guess it's time that I go back inside and get dressed for the day."

"Yeah," he agrees. "It's time to go home."

Home. That one word has changed meaning for me so many times. When I first joined the crew, home was a small, southern city along the coast of Italy. Then, it became this ship. Now, as I look up into the eyes of the goddess in front of me, home is her and wherever she takes me.

thirty-one
VETTE

PANIC SPEARS through me when I wake up alone. I open my eyes and sit straight up in bed looking around, but I don't see Alessandro. My mind immediately plays through a million scenarios. Maybe I've gone crazy, and he was a dream. Maybe he was only here for his vengeance, and then his soul moved onto its final resting place. Or, and this is the thought that hurt the most, he just used me to get his revenge. Then, I hear his voice like a siren's song calling me to the balcony.

He stands there, his hands on the banister, like an Olympic god looking down on Earth. A cacophony of sounds comes from the port we're docked beside, but it's his voice I focus on. He's talking to someone. No, that can't be right. Who would he be talking to out on the balcony? I don't feel his anger, and we're not touching. I open the door thinking maybe he's arguing with himself still, like he was last night. Then I hear a tiny voice from the balcony next door.

I greet them both and exchange introductions with the small child. I can barely see him through the slats from my angle, but since I'm not wearing any clothes, I can't step outside. I can, however, see his eyes shining brightly. I smile at the conversation Alessandro has with Jonah about my name. Ever since he learned what it means, Alessandro's refused to use the shortened version, letting all the syllables roll off his tongue. I love the way it sounds on his lips, and I want to reach for him and pull him in for a kiss. Then, I remember the small boy he's talking to.

How? How is that happening? I open and close my mouth. There are so many questions I want to ask but can't in front of Jonah. Alessandro doesn't appear ruffled by the situation. Is it possible he doesn't realize what's happening? He has to, right? I close the door without a word and sit on the closest chair. When I hear the handle turn, I see Alessandro walking through the open door, and my jaw drops. He sees me staring at him, and his expression goes from content to worried in an instant.

He drops to his knees in front of me. "Bella, are you okay?"

Again, my mouth opens and closes like a fish. I flounder, unsure what to say. Speech seems impossible, so I reach out a hand and place it on his cheek. The familiar undercurrent courses between us, and I take a deep breath.

"You're scaring me. What's wrong?"

"Nothing's wrong," I finally say. "You...you..." Fuck, why can't I get the words out? "You just talked to that little boy."

"Yeah, he was super cute and had come outside to let his parents sleep."

"No, I mean yes. Yes, he's super cute, but you talked to him. You just opened the door and walked over the threshold." I banged my hand on the chair's arm for emphasis.

"I came back inside because you were awake," he says, still not registering what I'm saying.

"There is no anger in you. There's no anger in me. You talked to that little boy. You opened the door, and we weren't touching."

He sits back on his heels, eyes boring into mine, trying to

process my words. I see the moment realization settles in. He clutches his chest, eyes like saucers, before he stands and puts his hand on the glass window. His muscles strain as he tries to push through it. Then, he turns and walks across the room away from me to the closet. He opens each door and then closes them. He does the same with the bathroom and the hall door. When he slams the hall door shut, a sob leaves his chest, bringing tears to my eyes. I stand to go to him before he turns to look at me.

"Is this real?" he asks. Surprise, elation, and wariness are all evident on his face.

I don't know how to answer his question, but I also can't stop hope from sprouting in my chest. If Jonah could see him and talk to him… If he had to open a door to walk through it… A smile spreads across my face, and tears overflow their wells.

"I guess there's only one way to find out, Mr. Ghost. Let's go home."

ALESSANDRO

SIX MONTHS LATER.

Getting off the ship was a little harder at the end of the voyage than it had been on the island. I was no longer invisible. I had no keycard or ID. Thankfully, however, none of the crew recognized me after all these years. Very few still remained who had worked with me. When we realized I wouldn't be able to simply walk off undetected, my beautiful and smart Odveta had a brilliant plan for me to pose as Greg. We looked enough alike to fool them by saying I had gotten my hair cut at the first stop and my keycard had fallen off the side of the ship. The steward looked me up. No, he looked Greg up, asked me a few questions, and decided his picture looked enough like me to allow me access to the room.

We quickly packed up everything we could find to make it look like he had gotten off the ship. Thankfully, he left his passport and money in the room. After that, it was surprisingly easy to get through the port. We left separately and took one of the shuttles to the airport. The hardest part was holding it together while separated from Odveta. She was, and remains, my lifeline.

I kiss the top of her head where she's asleep in the seat next to me. The past few months have been a whirlwind, and exhaustion seemed to set in as soon as our flight took off. I had to ditch Gregory's identity almost as soon as we got back to her house. That meant I needed a new one. Somehow, Odveta's family's connections were able to get me new copies of all of my actual identification. My birth certificate and my passport are in Odveta's bag under the seat.

Though I had warned her that the ships cover themselves by saying we disembarked in outside ports, Odveta was surprised to find I was never reported as missing. My personal items, including my ID, were never sent home to my family. I was just taken off payroll, and my body was dumped somewhere. I imagine they did the same thing with Samuel's charred remains. They didn't, however, subject Jaison, Francesca, and Constance to the same fate. They were sent home with apologies and condolences for the faulty wiring that has since been replaced. Arthur and Tony were reported as missing by the company.

Tracy was a godsend. Her bruises and story of Arthur's attack left everyone believing Greg went into hiding for having something to do with one or both of the other men's disappearances. Her story about having to rescue Odveta from the bar to sleep off the drugs she'd been given took all the scrutiny off of her. Since Tracy hadn't actually seen me, other than the quick glimpse of my form flashing into view as we left her room, I became nothing more than someone Odveta met on the trip home.

Now, we're on our way to Italy to see my nonna. My parents passed away when I was a child, and my nonna raised my sister and I. She had been so excited when I got the job with the cruise line. I would get to travel and live a life outside of our small town, something she'd never done. When I stopped writing and calling, she'd become worried, but there was nothing she could do besides wait for me to contact her. There was no one for her to call for information. We both cried when I made the first phone call home. Odveta held me while I sobbed when I found out that my sister got married last year and is pregnant with her first child. We'll be there when she gives birth.

Odveta stirs slightly, smiling up at me before falling back asleep. She continues to shock me with her intelligence and compassion, and she sets me on fire with her desire. I don't know what the future may bring for us, but I know life doesn't exist without her. My heart is full knowing that whatever comes our way, loving my sweet vengeance will be my life's purpose.

leya layne

Follow Leya all over social media:
https://linktr.ee/LeyaLayneAuthor

See her website for forthcoming releases and trigger/content warnings:
https://bisabelwrites.com/leyas-content-is-for-18-only/

Coming Soon

November 2024:Snowed-In in Cole County: A Cozy Romance Anthology

January 2025: Drenched in Cole County: A Cozy Romance Anthology

February 2025: Clarissa and the Wallflower

www.ingramcontent.com/pod-product-compliance
Lightning Source LLC
Chambersburg PA
CBHW031625310726

48974CB00003B/816